"I CAN'T O
"As soon a
shipping ou
Washington.

Wendy thrust her chin out in a gesture he was becoming very familiar with. "I'm not looking for a long-term relationship," she said. "But I'm scared and feeling all alone, and you're real and warm and solid, and I just . . . I just need you tonight. Stay here with me. One night."

One night. A promise of eight or ten or twelve hours of incredible delight. "And then we both walk away?"

"Do we have any other choice?"

"No." But maybe, he thought, if he indulged every fantasy he'd had about Wendy—and he'd entertained plenty—he could get over his fixation on her.

"Make up your mind," she said, crossing her arms. "I don't make this sort of offer every day."

Ah, hell, he already knew what his answer was. "You drive a hard bargain, lady," he said, reaching for her.

WHAT ARE *LOVESWEPT* ROMANCES?

They are stories of true romance and touching emotion. We believe those two very important ingredients are constants in our highly sensual and very believable stories in the LOVE-SWEPT line. Our goal is to give you, the reader, stories of consistently high quality that may sometimes make you laugh, sometimes make you cry, but are always fresh and creative and contain many delightful surprises within their pages.

Most romance fans read an enormous number of books. Those they truly love, they keep. Others may be traded with friends and soon forgotten. We hope that each LOVESWEPT romance will be a treasure—a "keeper." We will always try to publish

**LOVE STORIES YOU'LL NEVER FORGET
BY AUTHORS YOU'LL ALWAYS REMEMBER**

The Editors

HOT PROPERTY

KAREN LEABO

BANTAM BOOKS
NEW YORK · TORONTO · LONDON · SYDNEY · AUCKLAND

HOT PROPERTY
A Bantam Book / October 1998

ISBN 0-553-44653-3

Published simultaneously in the United States and Canada

Bantam Books are published by Bantam Books, a division of Bantam Dou-
bleday Dell Publishing Group, Inc. Its trademark, consisting of the words
"Bantam Books" and the portrayal of a rooster, is Registered in U.S.
Patent and Trademark Office and in other countries. Marca Registrada.
Bantam Books, 1540 Broadway, New York, New York 10036.

PRINTED IN THE UNITED STATES OF AMERICA

OPM   10 9 8 7 6 5 4 3 2 1

PROLOGUE

Turning thirty was tough, Wendy Thayer mused glumly as she waited forever at a traffic light on Lemmon Avenue.

First, there was the new laugh line she'd seen while looking in her mirror that morning. It had displayed incredibly bad timing by showing up on her birthday.

Second, there was James and his gift of a gold electroplated bracelet. When she'd opened the box during their rushed lunch date, it had been clear—so clear—what had gone through his mind in picking out her combination birthday/I'm-dumping-you gift.

What's the least amount of money I can spend and still save face?

The answer was $12.95, on sale at Lux Warehouse Jewelry. She'd seen the ad the day before when she'd been clipping coupons for her clients.

The light turned green and Wendy shifted into first gear. She felt remarkably unperturbed at getting dumped. Boyfriends were just too much trouble. The door dent in her brand-new Born to Shop company van was more upsetting.

At least she could look forward to her next client.

Barnie Neff was the sweetest little old man, a shut-in with severe arthritis and emphysema. Three months earlier he'd called her after seeing her ad on cable TV. He'd needed someone to pick out some library books for him.

He'd quickly become a regular customer, despite his humble lifestyle. She had recently expanded her personal-shopping business to include errands, and Mr. Neff often gave her unusual tasks, like delivering a box of old books to a dealer for appraisal, or taking his ancient radio to a repair shop. Once he'd had her deliver some old blankets to a homeless shelter. Today her job was more mundane—laundry, cold medicine, and a new pair of house slippers.

Mr. Neff's rickety frame house stood about as straight as a drunken sailor, and it hadn't seen paint in so long, Wendy couldn't determine the original color. But inside it was always cozy and comfortable. Wendy pulled up to the curb, collected Mr. Neff's laundry from the back of her van, and headed for the front porch.

"Come on in, sweetie," Mr. Neff called to her before she'd even rung the bell.

She pushed open the door. The scent of banana bread hung invitingly in the air. He must be having a good day, Wendy concluded. When he was feeling up to it, he liked to bake bread.

Mr. Neff hobbled out of the kitchen to greet her, dragging along his oxygen tank. He wore a frilly apron tied around his fragile waist and a smudge of flour on his nose.

"Hiya, sweetie!" he said. "Look at that laundry. You do too much, you know. I'll bet you don't take laundry home for your other clients."

"You're special," Wendy said, putting down the laundry basket and leaning over to give Mr. Neff a peck on the cheek. "The slippers are blue—that was the only color in your size. But they were on sale."

"Sure, sure, anything's fine." He examined the slippers sitting on top of the laundry and nodded, satisfied.

"And the cold medicine is the nondrowsy kind. I had a fifty-cent coupon."

"Cold medicine." He made a production of coughing. "You're in the nick of time with that stuff."

"You must not be feeling too bad if you're in the kitchen."

"Oh, well, it comes and goes. What's the damage?" He reached into his back pocket for his wallet.

"Twenty-three fifty," she said, handing him a piece of paper bearing a complete accounting of her work and the charges.

He studied the accounting a moment. "For the slippers and the cold medicine, maybe, but that laundry was hard work. Come on, now, charge me a fair price."

"Twenty-three fifty," she insisted. "I threw the

laundry in with mine. It was hardly any trouble at all, and I did charge you for it."

He laboriously counted out exact change and handed it to her. "You're a bargain, sweetie. Don't know how I ever did without you. Now, before you rush off, I have a special errand for you. Have a seat on the divan, I'll be right back."

Wendy cleared some magazines off the threadbare brown sofa and sat down, then looked at her watch. She hoped whatever errand Mr. Neff had in mind wouldn't take long.

He reappeared shortly bearing a stack of velvet boxes. "Wait till you get a load of these." Then he opened the first box, and Wendy could feel her eyes bulging. Nestled on a satin lining was the most beautiful sapphire necklace she'd ever seen. The three gems that comprised the teardrop design were at least one carat each, a deep midnight blue cut in the old style and set in an art deco platinum setting.

"Oh, it's lovely."

"It was my mother's. All of these things were hers. But . . . no sense in leaving them in a drawer to collect dust." He opened another box to reveal a diamond and pearl bracelet; another carried two dinner rings, one a ruby surrounded by baguette diamonds, one a square-cut emerald flanked by two oval-cut diamonds. Mr. Neff continued to open boxes and set them on the coffee table for her inspection.

"Try them on if you like."

"Oh, no, I'm afraid I'd be tempted to slip one into

my purse. They're beautiful." She ran one finger over the finely detailed links of a silver chain.

"I've found a buyer. John Winstead at the Gold and Diamond Trade Mart on Maple. You deliver 'em, he'll give 'em a quick eyeball—"

"You're selling these beautiful heirlooms?"

"Look, sweetie, I got no daughters or sisters, and I ain't gonna wear 'em myself." He laughed a little at his own joke. "I'm okay financially, but I can use the money."

"Why doesn't this Mr. Winstead come here?"

"Frankly, I didn't want him to see where I live. Might drive down the price."

"Oh. Well, this is beyond my normal services. . . ."

"You're bonded and insured, aren't you? Anyway, I'll make it worth your while."

He opened one final box. In it was the loveliest pair of diamond stud earrings Wendy had ever seen. "You keep these for yourself."

"Oh, no, I couldn't accept such an extravagant—"

Mr. Neff started laughing. "You don't think they're real, do you? I'm not that crazy. They're strictly costume. But Mother wore them a lot. I'd be pleased to know they're being enjoyed by someone like you, someone nice." He paused, then got a little misty. "Mother would have liked you. Have I told you you look a lot like my younger sister, God rest her soul?"

Only about a dozen times. "All right, I'll accept the

earrings. And thank you." She gave him a hug, wishing all of Born to Shop's clients were as sweet.

The old man waited until the sound of Wendy Thayer's van faded into the stillness of the early spring afternoon. Then he whipped off the stupid apron and pulled the oxygen tubes out of his nose. "Coast is clear," he called in a voice suddenly stronger.

Two burly men appeared from upstairs, each of them loaded down with empty packing boxes. With practiced efficiency, they began packing up the knick-knacks. The old man could feel it in his bones—it was time to clear out, for good this time. Another couple of days and he'd be on his way to Tahiti.

He picked up the phone.

"Three-two-oh," a bland male voice answered.

"The hook's set," the old man said. "The fish will be at the rendezvous at the agreed-upon time. Wait until you receive confirmation that the funds have been deposited before taking further action."

"Understood."

With an unfamiliar twinge of conscience, the old man added, "Oh, and don't let the fish suffer, okay? Make it clean."

"I always work clean."

He hung up, again without any small talk, and sighed. Wendy was the best pack mule he'd ever used. Who could suspect that face, those big green eyes? But she was also a nice girl. She *did* look like his sister. He would miss her.

ONE

Turning thirty-five was hell, Michael Taggert thought as he stretched and tried to work the kinks out of his back. His body told him he wasn't a kid anymore. Stakeouts, even short ones, made his muscles ache. If he missed his morning run, he noticed. Even coffee, which he used to drink by the gallon, made him jittery now.

"Feeling your age, old man?"

"Don't rub it in, Joe. Or I'll start making bald jokes."

Michael's partner, Joe Gaglione, laughed and rubbed his shiny head. "Wait'll you get to be my age. Baldness is the least of my worries. Hell, I'd gladly look like Kojak if I could ditch the low-fat diet. Then there's the dental work—I'm lookin' at dentures in ten years if I'm not careful. Don't even get me started on my prostate—"

"Joe, please. My birthday is depressing enough without you reminding me of what's to come."

Joe laughed again. "Aw, you're still a kid. In twenty years, when you're my age, you'll look back at this day and wonder what you were bitching about." He gulped down the last of his coffee.

Joe was right, Michael acknowledged. He was still young enough that the FBI wanted him—had actually recruited him. If they accepted his application, he wouldn't be spending the rest of his life as a lowly sergeant in the Theft Division of the Dallas Police Department.

He'd hoped to make an arrest on the Art Deco Museum case by his birthday. Cases came and went, but this one had been stuck in his craw for longer than most. His lack of progress on the six-month-old jewel and art heist had become a bone of contention between himself and his captain. Solving the case would look good on his résumé.

Today, though, he was about to turn a corner. According to his snitch, who worked at the Gold and Diamond Trade Mart, something big was going down, some kind of substantial off-the-books delivery.

"Anything happening in there?" Joe asked.

Michael peered through his binoculars into the main showroom of the Trade Mart. "Our bad boy is working the counter closest to the door." The "bad boy" was the fence ID'd by Michael's snitch.

"And our snitch?"

"Right at his elbow." The snitch had promised to

call Michael the moment he spotted anything suspicious. Everything was in place.

"You get an invite to Patterson's retirement party?" Joe asked in a bored voice.

"Yeah. I heard everyone who ever worked for him got one. You going?"

"Hell, yeah. I've never seen the mayor's mansion. You?"

Michael shook his head and shrugged, shooting new waves of pain through his back. He needed a good massage therapist.

A white van with green lettering pulled into a parking spot near the Trade Mart's front door.

"Born to Shop?" Michael read off the side of the van.

"Yeah, haven't you heard of them? Rich people who don't have time hire these ladies to do their shopping and run errands. They got ads all over cable TV."

"I don't watch TV, and if I ever saw an ad for something like that, I'd forget it as soon as possible. Sheesh." He paused, thinking about the concept a moment. "My ex-wife could have started a company like that."

"Oh, yeah. Faye. Born to shop, all right."

"Problem was, she wasn't born to pay for it all." The thought of all those credit card bills made Michael's skin crawl. He'd escaped from Faye just in time to avoid bankruptcy and had spent the last seven years paying off her debts.

The van's door opened and a young woman

climbed out. The first thing Michael noticed about her was how the March wind caught the hem of her short skirt and lifted it just far enough for him to get a glimpse of pale pink panties.

"She matches the description those homeless guys gave us," Joe said.

Michael brought his hormones into line and paid attention to what really mattered. The woman was petite, about five foot two, maybe 110 pounds, with auburn hair piled on top of her head. Oval face. Full, pouty lips. Legs up to her armpits, shown to perfection by a short blue dress. She wore clogs on her feet.

He'd bet her eyes were green. "Yeah, she matches, all right."

"I'm calling in her plates."

While Joe consulted Records for the van's registered owner, Michael watched the woman, fascinated. Wow. Could she possibly be the brazen hussy who'd been selling hot merchandise all over town, always one step ahead of the cops? The description sure didn't do her justice.

"Damn."

"Something happening?" Joe asked, squinting through the tinted glass of their surveillance van.

"No, she's just gorgeous . . . uh-oh."

"Uh-oh, what?"

"She just pulled a big shopping bag from the van. Looks like she's delivering something."

Joe hung up the cellular and read from the notes he'd just taken. "Van's registered to a corporate entity, Born to Shop."

"Might have guessed she'd shield herself behind a corporate veil."

The woman walked into the Trade Mart at a fast, efficient clip, then immediately struck up a conversation with the fence. The cellular rang. Michael picked it up.

"The girl who just came in," the snitch whispered. "She's got deco jewelry—boxes of it. I gotta go." He hung up.

Michael turned to Joe. "Work on the search warrant, okay? Let's haul in the fence. I'm following Miss Born to Shop."

"Wait, I thought I was gonna follow the suspect."

Michael winked. "That was before I got a good look at her."

In twenty seconds flat he was in his car, parked nearby. The woman came out within a couple of minutes and got into her van. She didn't look hurried or hassled. In fact, she paused before pulling out of her parking space to read something, then made a note before donning her sunglasses.

Cool cookie, Michael thought. He couldn't wait to find out what her story was.

Wendy pulled into a spot close to the bank's front door, then walked right up to a teller. Amazing, considering it was five minutes to three. Any later and she'd have been holding on to this ridiculous wad of cash overnight.

Mr. Neff hadn't said anything about cash, she thought, exasperated.

The teller smiled sweetly. "Can I help you?"

"Yes, I'd like to deposit this money into this account." She handed the teller a fat envelope along with the deposit slip Mr. Neff had prepared.

The teller counted the cash, then started punching buttons on her machine.

"Wait."

Wendy jumped at the terse command coming from behind her. She whirled around, thinking someone was trying to butt in line, ready to give the rude interloper a piece of her mind. When she saw the man, however, all her words died in her throat. He was big, he was gorgeous, and he looked mad enough to chew her up and spit her out for fertilizer.

It was the mad part that reduced her to silence. That and the law enforcement shield he had in his hand, identifying him as Detective Sergeant Michael Taggert.

"Excuse me, sir?" the teller asked, looking bewildered.

The stranger grabbed Wendy's arm with one powerful hand and slapped handcuffs over her wrist.

"This woman is under arrest for transport of stolen goods. I'll need that cash she was about to deposit as evidence."

Now the teller looked truly alarmed. "I'll get the manager."

Wendy finally found her voice. "Are you out of your mind?" she asked the detective. "What is it you think I've stolen, you moron? You've obviously got the wrong person. Now uncuff me *right now.*"

The cop had the nerve to smile at her. "You won't get free for a long, long time if I have anything to say about it."

"You're making a big mistake," she said, speaking through her gritted teeth and smiling. Perhaps all the people staring at them would think this was a prank. "I'm a member of the Chamber of Commerce. I know the mayor personally. I'm a taxpayer. My tax dollars pay—"

He repeated the last part with her. "—pay my salary, I know. Believe me, lady, I've heard it all." He pulled a card from his pocket. "You have the right to remain silent—"

"Like hell. Who exactly do you think I am?"

"—if you choose to give up that right, anything you say—"

"I know the spiel. I watch TV too. What have I done?"

"—can and will be used against you . . ." He went on, oblivious to her ranting. She soon found both her hands cuffed behind her. She was escorted in this humiliating fashion to the branch manager's office.

No help there. The officious manager handed the cop her deposit slip and Mr. Neff's cash and hustled them out a back door in an effort to avoid bad publicity.

"I'll never bank here again!" she called out over her shoulder as Michael Taggert dragged her away.

"No great threat, since you'll be in jail," the detective said as he stuffed her into the back seat of a bland four-door sedan.

Okay, deep breaths, Wendy told herself. Think about this for a minute. She was the victim of mistaken identity. As soon as this Neanderthal took her to the station or downtown or wherever, the cops would immediately realize the error of their ways and let her go with big fat apologies.

She would have grounds for a huge lawsuit, she mused. But instead of asking for money, she would demand that Sergeant Michael Taggert crawl on his oh-so-handsome hands and knees and beg forgiveness.

This pleasant little fantasy lasted only as long as it took to clear the bank parking lot. The cop's car was making the most god-awful sounds.

"Does this car have a muffler?" she asked as they chugged along in the thickening traffic. Late afternoon was a bad time to be heading downtown. "It sounds terrible."

"I'm sure it has a muffler."

"Oh, you're not taking the Tollway, are you? Harry Hines is faster."

He ignored her advice and headed for the Tollway. "I got to hand it to you, you do cute real well."

"I'm not trying—" She stopped. What was the point? She was trying to be helpful. That's what she was programmed to do. That was what she loved to do. Some people just didn't appreciate it.

A new thought occurred to her. "Is it my van?" she asked. Everything about the sale last week had seemed legitimate at the time, but she'd gotten a deal on her new company vehicle that had seemed almost too good to be true.

Taggert put on the brakes and, instead of entering the Tollway, turned onto a side street. He switched off the engine. He waited. If the silence was supposed to make Wendy want to spill her guts, it was working.

"I've got all the paperwork at the office," she said, desperation creeping into her voice. "Don't you want to see it?"

"Lady," he finally said, "you are in a heap of trouble. Frankly, you look too smart for the dumb act to be convincing. So why don't you knock it off and tell me who you're working for?"

She sat up straighter and met his all-too-direct gaze in the rearview mirror. "I'm self-employed."

"Then you're a damn good thief."

She sighed. They were talking in circles.

"Listen, miss, I can't make you any promises or cut you any deals. Only the D.A. can do that. But I can assure you of one thing. This process will go a lot easier for you if you cooperate from the beginning. So let's start over. Where'd you get the bankroll?"

"The bankroll . . . well, why didn't you ask that in the first place?" Now they were getting somewhere! "That's Mr. Neff's money. Oh. Okay, I see." Her brain clicked as everything fell into place. This had nothing to do with her van. "The jewelry. You're telling me the jewelry Mr. Neff gave me to sell is hot?"

"Duh."

"If you would just say what you mean instead of

trying to be clever and intimidate me, we could have cleared this up a long time ago! Barnie Neff is a client of mine. He's a shut-in, and I run errands for him. He gave me his mother's jewelry to deliver to the guy at the Gold and Diamond Trade Mart. No way is it stolen."

The cop whipped out a notebook and started scribbling. "Neff? N-E-F-F?" He stopped writing and extended his arm, then stretched his neck to one side and the other, as if he had a backache.

"Yes," she answered, watching the play of muscles along his shoulders and upper arm. Her body tensed with unwelcome awareness of the fact that her adversary was male—very male.

"You run errands for him?"

"I just told you that. It's what I do for a living."

"And you go to his house?" Taggert asked hopefully.

"Yes. He lives at 2824 Monty Avenue. But surely you don't think Mr. Neff is some kind of criminal."

"Let me put it this way. That nice man in the store who bought the jewelry from you? He's a well-known fence with a record as long as your legs."

"Don't you mean arm?"

"Yeah, as long as your arm. That's what I said."

She decided not to argue with him, but she made a mental note: Detective Michael Taggert had noticed her legs. The knowledge gave her a guilty thrill and a small sense of . . . power? He wasn't as cold to her as he pretended.

He hunched his shoulders and bent his head forward again. She could almost feel his discomfort herself. "I know a good massage therapist," she offered.

He turned around to give her a look she couldn't quite read. Had she said something wrong? Then he shrugged, winced at the pain, and turned away from her. He grabbed a cellular phone from somewhere and dialed with a series of quick jabs.

"Michael Taggert here, Theft Division? Yeah, I need you to check out an address for me." He repeated the address she'd given him.

"Mr. Neff is a harmless little old man," Wendy tried again. "He's on oxygen. He never leaves the house."

"You better hope he's not harmless. 'Cause he's your ticket out of jail."

Michael tried not to feel sorry for Wendy Thayer as he watched her go through the booking process. So she'd grown up without a father. So she didn't have anything more alarming on her record than a couple of parking tickets. She was also a struggling business owner who'd suddenly started making money.

He'd tried to question her further about her dealings with this mysterious Mr. Neff, but she'd asked for a lawyer, so he'd had to quit. She'd made her phone call and claimed the lawyer was on his way.

To her credit, she didn't cry or whine the way a lot of women did when they were fingerprinted and had mug shots taken. She held her chin up, and at every opportunity she stared daggers at him.

But every so often her lower lip trembled, sending shots of awareness right to his core. She was beautiful. No matter what she'd done, she caused a response in him at the cellular level.

After an eternity she was brought to an interrogation room and left to stew while they waited for her attorney. Michael watched her through the two-way mirror. She paced, she bit one fingernail down to the quick, she sighed.

How could someone with everything she had going for her turn to crime? She hadn't grown up in the projects. She wasn't a drug addict or a single mother with babies to feed and no job. He supposed she was drawn by the thrill.

When her lawyer showed up, Michael wasn't surprised to see that it was Nathaniel Mondell, a high-priced defense attorney favored by white-collar criminals and tax-fraud artists all over the Metroplex. The fact that Wendy had those kinds of connections was just another indication of her guilt, as far as Michael was concerned.

Too bad. A part of him wished she was just some sucker who'd been duped into taking the risk for the real thief. But she seemed too smart for that. Besides, there were the earrings they'd found in her purse.

After giving her a few minutes alone with the lawyer, Michael entered the interrogation room. He shook hands with Mondell, whose pleasant round face and pale, blinking eyes behind thick glasses hid a sharp legal mind.

Michael set up the recorder. They covered the basics—name, address, age.

"Wait a minute," he said. "Your birthday's today?"

"Yeah, and this isn't how I'd planned on celebrating," she replied tartly.

"Hmm. I'll be damned."

"What?"

"Uh, nothing." The last thing he wanted was to bond with his suspect because they shared a birthday. This was a first, though. He shook his head and got right down to it. He was known for his lightning-quick, killer interrogations.

"We checked out the address you gave us on Monty. The house was completely empty, abandoned. Still want to stick with your story?"

After flashing a look of bewilderment, Wendy glanced over at Mondell and shrugged. "I must've given you the wrong house number. I was upset—"

"Try again."

"Look, Mr. Neff was there this afternoon. He was baking banana bread."

"Uh-huh."

"He had a brown sofa and a rug with pink flowers and a, a telephone. Electricity. Yes, that's it." She turned to Mondell. "You can check the utility records, can't you?"

Mondell smiled indulgently. "We'll check all of this out, don't worry."

"Okay, suppose I take your word for it," Michael said. "This Neff guy was there, but he moved out in a hurry. How do you explain these?" He plunked a small velvet box onto the table.

"I, um, uh-oh."

"Wendy," the lawyer cautioned.

"Those are some earrings Mr. Neff gave to me as payment. He said they were rhinestones or something. . . ."

Michael could tell by the look of dread on Wendy's face that she knew what was coming.

"They're real?" she squeaked.

"Worth about four grand," Michael said casually. "Pretty good pay for running a few errands."

He was just about to congratulate himself for scoring a point when the door opened. No knock, no apology. Michael whirled around. "What the hell . . ."

His voice trailed off. Standing just inside the doorway was a man whose square face he knew well. From newspapers. From TV. But never at the police station.

"Hello, Nate," the newcomer said to Wendy's lawyer. "Glad you could get here so quickly." Then he turned to Michael. "Are you the man responsible for Wendy Thayer's arrest?"

Michael stood up and faced the man. "Yes, Mr. Mayor. Sir."

"There's been a mistake." Clifford Munn, Dallas's mayor, was an imposing figure of a man with clean, chiseled features, gently graying hair, and a real expensive power suit. He also could thunder when he wanted to.

"She delivered stolen museum pieces to a fence,"

Michael tried to explain. "I saw that with my own eyes."

"It's a mistake," Munn said again, a bit calmer now. "I know this woman. She shops for my wife. We're having a party in one week. A big party."

Ah, yes. The retirement party for Captain Patterson, a forty-five-year veteran of the department.

"If Wendy's in jail," the mayor continued, "she can't shop for the party, can she?"

"Well, no, sir." Michael resisted the urge to tug at his collar, which suddenly felt tight.

"If Wendy can't do the shopping, my wife will have a nervous breakdown. What's your name?"

"Sergeant Michael Taggert." Michael didn't add the "sir" this time. He did not deserve to be dressed down as if he were a green Police Academy grad just because the mayor was having a party.

Munn narrowed his eyes. "You've applied to the Bureau."

"Yes, sir." Oh, great. How did hizzonor know that? Wait a minute. Michael remembered the campaign promises now. Clifford Munn. Tough on Crime. Former FBI special agent, retired on disability after being injured in the line of duty. Damn, damn, damn.

"I keep my hand in things," he said, answering Michael's unasked question. "Listen, Mr. FBI Wannabe. Wendy Thayer isn't a criminal. You straighten this out in time for my party, or I'll personally see to it your application keeps an appointment with a paper shredder." He turned and slammed the door on his way out, giving Michael no chance to react, no chance to defend himself.

He looked over at Wendy. She was actually smiling. The shark attorney was trying not to laugh. And suddenly the whole tone of the interrogation changed. Michael no longer held all the cards.

"I told you I knew the mayor," she said. "So what do you say you quit harassing me and let me help you find Mr. Neff?"

TWO

Michael's police-issue sedan sputtered like an antique tractor as he started it up the next morning at the crack of dawn. All right, so Wendy Thayer was right about the muffler.

What an awesome creature that woman was. In all his umpteen years in law enforcement, he'd never encountered a suspect as alluring as Wendy—or as unlikely. He'd like to believe she was innocent. But there was too much smoke coming from her direction.

His car coughed and died. Gritting his teeth with determination, as if that could somehow help the ailing car, Michael started it up again. Sometime that day he'd have to turn the car over to the motor pool for repairs and get a loaner.

But not now. Now he had to drive over to the Southeast Station and track down the two patrol officers who'd checked out the house on Monty. About the only chance he had of catching them and questioning them in person was to grab them on their way out of their morning briefing, before they hit the streets.

His thoughts turned to Wendy again during the short, pre-rush-hour drive east on I-30. He'd been too eager to pin the theft on her, he decided. She was the first, the only, real break he'd had on the Art Deco Museum case, and he badly wanted to mark this one solved. Not that he believed she was a blameless pawn. No one who shopped for a living could be innocent, and she was too smart to be a mere pawn.

But she had to be working for someone. If he could catch that someone, and Wendy turned state's evidence against him or her, it would be a win-win situation. Michael would have a feather in his cap, and Wendy would probably get off with a slap on the wrist, making the mayor happy.

Of course, Wendy's business would be in a shambles, he thought with a twinge of guilt. Which of her customers would ever trust her again? Then he marveled at the workings of the male mind when confronted with hormones. If she was a thief or a fence or a pack mule, she *deserved* to lose her business. He had no reason to feel guilty for doing his job, despite the number Mayor Munn had tried to lay on him.

The Southeast Station was a hive of activity as the night shift gave way to the day. Michael found a parking place, showed his badge at the front desk, then slipped into the small auditorium where officers were briefed before starting their patrols. As soon as he identified the captain in charge, he approached and made his request.

"Gonzales is in the break room," the captain said amiably. "I just saw him."

"Thanks."

Michael followed the smell of stale coffee to a small break room where a knot of blue-uniformed officers scarfed pastries and laughed at an off-color joke. He remembered with fondness the days of street patrol, the camaraderie, the black humor.

"Gonzales?" he asked the group.

"Right here," a young, barrel-chested man said. "I'm Gonzales. You must be Detective Taggert. Is there a problem?"

"No, not really," Michael assured him. The other officers left him and Gonzales in private. "I just wanted a little more detail on that house you checked out for me."

"On Monty," the officer confirmed. "Not much to tell. It was completely empty, clean as a whistle."

"Were the utilities on?" Michael asked, taking a cue from Wendy's question during the interrogation.

"Yeah. The lights worked. But there was no sign that the place was occupied. If any kids or homeless people had been shacking up there, we'd know it. In fact . . ." Gonzales paused to remember. "The place was unnaturally clean. No junk mail or newspapers stacking up, either."

Michael jotted that down in his notebook. It wasn't much. "Anything else? Even something that doesn't seem important?"

Gonzales hesitated. "This is gonna sound stupid. But I swear, I smelled banana bread in the kitchen."

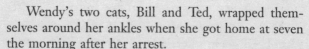

Wendy's two cats, Bill and Ted, wrapped themselves around her ankles when she got home at seven the morning after her arrest.

"I can't walk," she complained, trying to nudge them aside as she closed the front door behind her and set down her purse. "It's only been one day. You have dry food available. You can't be that hungry."

They were, and they let her know it. Bill started gnawing on her clog, and Ted jumped up on the coat tree in her entry hall and tried to climb onto her shoulder. They yowled in harmony.

"Blame Michael Taggert, not me," she groused as she herded her brood into the kitchen, praying she had another couple of cans of food in the cupboard. "He's the one who testified at my arraignment and made me sound like a conniving felon."

Wendy was convinced it was Taggert's fault the judge had set her bail at an unreasonable hundred grand. She'd had to come up with 10 percent in order to post bond—not an easy feat given that she'd pumped all of her assets into Born to Shop.

"Here, chicken livers and gizzards, your favorite flavor." She dumped two cans of smelly cat food into Bill and Ted's bowls, which silenced the yowling. Frenzied purring accompanied her as she left the kitchen and headed into the bathroom. She had just enough time to shower, dress, and drive to the office before her employees started arriving.

On the way out the front door fifteen minutes later

she began mentally organizing her workday and the tasks to be delegated. Without breaking stride she grabbed her newspaper from the front walk, then chucked it into the back of the van. Maybe she could read it later. First she had to figure out how to clear her name. She didn't believe she could trust the good detective to find the real thief, since he was so convinced she was the guilty party.

Wendy opened the window to her van and let her hair air-dry as she drove the ten minutes from her garden apartment in North Dallas to her storefront office in the Preston Royal shopping center. She'd thought long and hard before relocating from her spare bedroom to this uptown address—she paid some of the highest rent in the Metroplex. But the additional visibility, combined with her cable TV ads, was paying off. She was finally making some serious money. Her goal, once she got her small-business loans paid off, was to give herself a fat raise.

Now that goal seemed a long way off. Mounting a legal defense against these spurious theft charges—especially since her attorney was notoriously pricey—wouldn't be cheap.

She tried hard to push her problems aside as she pulled into a parking space under Born to Shop's green-striped awning. No matter what was going on in her life, she had to keep the business functional and efficient. Customers gave you one chance in this business. She'd discovered the hard way that if she was later than promised, if she forgot anything, she wouldn't get a call back.

Let's see, today was a dog-walking day, she remembered. Before she got out of the van, she consulted her electronic organizer: Mrs. Frazier's Pomeranians, Mr. Damian's rottweiler. She could probably delegate the poms to one of her employees, but the rotty was hers alone. No one else could deal with him.

A tap on her window distracted her. She looked up. Her heart gave a jump of recognition, then sank. Michael Taggert was scowling at her through the closed passenger window. Idly she wondered what that gorgeous face of his would look like graced with a smile.

She ran the window down. "I just got out of jail an hour ago," she snapped. "If you want to take me back, you'll have to catch me first." She put her hand on her keys, still stuck in the ignition, and glared at him, daring him to whip out his handcuffs.

"I'm not here to arrest you."

"Then why—"

"Can we go inside, maybe have a cup of coffee?"

He sounded almost . . . what, hopeful? Wendy found that hard to believe. Where was the arrogance, the superior attitude?

"If you want privacy, my office isn't the place," she said cautiously. "Besides, I don't want to advertise my predicament to my employees." As dear as they all were to her, like her own family almost, they were as prone to the temptations of gossip as anyone. She couldn't afford for any of her clients to find out she was a jailbird. They trusted her with their cars, their housekeys, sometimes even their children.

She unlocked the door. Without hesitation Michael climbed into her van, filling it with his overwhelming presence. Funny, she'd thought the van extraordinarily roomy until now.

"I saw a convenience store around the corner," he said. "I'll spring for the coffee."

She considered turning him down flat. But her curiosity overcame her. Why was he suddenly making nice? She restarted the van's engine and pulled out of her parking space. "The Exxon station down the block has better coffee, and it's only seventy-nine cents."

He nodded. "Then by all means, the Exxon station it is."

As she turned out of the parking lot, she sensed a restlessness beside her, something she couldn't put her finger on. Maybe he didn't like her driving. Some people, some men in particular, were nervous passengers. James, the macho jerk, she recalled with a frown, had refused to let her drive even when they took her car.

"I'm a good driver," she said. "You don't have to worry. I've never had an accident."

"A few parking tickets, though," he quipped. "But your driving doesn't bother me."

So. He'd checked up on her.

She pulled into the gas station. Neither she nor her reluctant host said anything as they entered the attached Snack Shop. Michael poured them two large coffees and paid for them at the window. Wendy doctored hers with cream and sugar. The silence continued until they returned to her van.

Wendy had never been known for her patience. "Okay, what's up? Why are you being so . . ." She struggled for the right word. *Nice* didn't cut it. ". . . so nonconfrontational?"

"As opposed to yesterday? Yesterday I was trying to browbeat a confession out of you. Today I'm not."

"Then what do you—"

"I want your help. I need your help. And you may not realize it, but you need mine. My testimony in a courtroom could make or break you."

She considered this. Mondell had warned her that Michael Taggert was a formidable opponent, particularly in open court. His performance at the arraignment was just a warm-up. What jurist could fail to be intimidated into believing anything he said? She decided Michael had a point.

"So you'll temper your testimony in exchange for . . ." She let her voice trail off as a series of X-rated thoughts crossed her mind. Surely he wasn't suggesting that! She'd heard such things happened all the time, but Michael didn't seem the type to have to manipulate a woman into . . . well, he wasn't suggesting that, was he?

She was horrified to discover that she didn't find the possibility as repugnant as it should have been. In fact, a telling warmth was spreading through her like butter on warm toast.

"You're blushing," Michael said. One corner of his mouth turned up in what might pass for a smile. That foreign expression on his face so disconcerted her that she couldn't respond for a moment.

He filled the silence. "I'm merely suggesting that you lead me to the person you work for. The D.A. isn't interested in prosecuting you if he can get the person responsible, the brains behind—"

She snapped back to reality. "I've told you a million times, I'm not working for some crime boss. Much as it pains me, I've come to the conclusion that sweet little Mr. Neff set me up to take the fall. So I'll do what I can to help you find him."

Michael sighed. "That would be a start."

"But you have to believe I'm innocent."

"No, I don't. I can't. I believe what the evidence tells me."

Now it was Wendy's turn to sigh. She supposed on the surface she looked guilty as hell. She'd have to settle for the fact that Michael was willing to believe she hadn't acted alone. "Did you check out the utilities for the house on Monty?" she asked.

He nodded. "The gas and electric were under the name Pat Walters. Whoever he or she is, they never called in a disconnect order or gave a forwarding address when they left."

"Pat Walters," Wendy repeated thoughtfully. "Maybe Mr. Neff rented, and Walters is his landlord."

"My partner is trying to track down this Walters person, but no luck so far. Can you give me a description of Mr. Neff?"

"Oh, yes." She'd thought hard about this during the long, sleepless night in jail. Thank goodness she had a good power of observation. "He was about five ten, in his mid-sixties, gray hair, thinning on top. He had bushy eyebrows, hazel eyes, a kind of sunken mouth—he didn't have many teeth."

Michael made notes. "What about his weight?"

"He was too thin. I'm not good at guessing weight, but he was frail and stooped. He had arthritis, so he had trouble getting around, and he was on oxygen. How far could a guy like that get?"

Michael looked at her thoughtfully for a moment, then shook his head. "Maybe you're more innocent than I thought," he murmured.

"Pardon me?" She didn't think she'd heard correctly.

"You. Innocent. Did it ever occur to you that your Mr. Neff might have been faking the illness? If he lied to you about his mother's jewelry, he could lie about anything."

"I hadn't thought of that," she admitted. She liked to think of herself as a hardheaded businesswoman, but more than one customer had led her down the garden path, rooking her into loads of work with no intention of paying her.

Suddenly she remembered how, when she'd seen him the day before, he'd seemed to be feeling great until she reminded him he had a cold. Then he'd abruptly started coughing. "He might have been faking the glasses too. And the gold tooth."

"Gold tooth?"

"Didn't I mention that?"

"No. You said he didn't have many teeth."

"He didn't. But one in front had a gold cap."

Michael made more notes in his pad. "What about scars and tattoos?"

She couldn't tell whether he was being facetious or not, so she answered him honestly. "Not that I recall."

He paused, thinking, and scratched his head with the end of his pen. Wendy watched in fascination as the black waves of his hair danced, then fell back into place.

"Would you be willing to work with a police artist?" he asked.

"Sure. When and where?"

"Now. She works downtown in the Physical Evidence Division. I'll drive you over there."

"I'd rather take my own car," she said. "I have a couple of errands I can run after I finish with the artist." She could pick up Mrs. Glover's restored painting from that little gallery in the Arts District. And Yoda the rottweiler was in Oak Lawn, which she could hit on her way back uptown.

"Do you need directions?" Michael asked, pulling her back into the present.

"Just an address. I'll find it. She held up her battered, beloved map book. Then she grabbed her electronic organizer from the dashboard, opened it, and turned it on.

"Seven eighteen Cantegral Street," he said as he pulled the door handle to let himself out. "I'll meet you there."

"Detective?"

He paused. "Huh?"

"Don't you want me to drive you back to your car?"

"Oh. Right." He slammed the door and managed, somehow, not to look foolish.

Wendy liked that about him. He was the most self-possessed, confident person she'd ever met. Still, she almost wished she'd let him get out and walk. Another five minutes so close to all that manliness, and her screaming hormones would become audible.

Michael felt like an idiot as he sat silently, finishing his coffee, while Wendy drove back to her storefront. How had he managed to forget that they'd driven three blocks from his car to get coffee? That was the problem. When he was around Wendy, his brain short-circuited.

He'd known it was a mistake when he'd climbed into the close confines of her van. The van *smelled* like her, a light, breezy fragrance as fresh as a spring morning and twice as intoxicating. He didn't know if it was perfume, soap, or just Wendy, but he couldn't seem to get his fill of it.

He'd tried to concentrate on his note taking, but every so often he had to look up at her. Even in the direct light of the morning sun, her face was as smooth as a child's, not a line or wrinkle in sight. Her auburn hair was pulled back in a youthful ponytail with a purple ribbon, showing off a long, slender neck.

Today she was wearing a short denim skirt and matching sleeveless vest, revealing enticing amounts of smooth, tanned arm and leg. Her dainty feet were encased in flat multicolored sandals. Her toenails were painted purple.

He'd never made love to a woman with purple toenails, he mused. And why in hell was he thinking about making love to this one? It wasn't as if that were even a remote possibility.

She pulled into the same parking spot, beneath a green-striped awning, that she'd left a few minutes ago. "I have to run inside and spend about ten minutes covering all the bases," she said. "Then I'll meet you there."

"You're not going to change your mind?" he asked warily, having been burned too many times by too many promises from suspects, witnesses, victims, and snitches alike. In general, he'd discovered, people didn't like dealing with police.

"No, I'll be there. If the artist can come up with a reasonable likeness of Mr. Neff, I'll pay to have it plastered all over town. I'll be ten minutes behind you."

With that she hopped out of the van, grabbed a tote bag and the organizer, and scurried inside.

Michael returned to his own car, shaking off a feeling he'd decided to label the "Wendy Thayer Effect." Had he been fantasizing about her toenails? One would think he'd never sat close to a beautiful woman before.

His ex, Faye, was beautiful, but she had a totally different look. Faye was polished, like a high-maintenance showhorse that had been freshly groomed. Wendy had a natural quality about her, as if she'd just been swimming in a mountain lake. Nude.

Oh, hell, he had to stop this—now. He climbed into his car and turned the key. The coughing and sputtering started up again, but the engine didn't. Start up, that is. Michael cranked and cranked for a good five minutes, but the damn thing just wouldn't catch.

Wendy peeked out the door, perplexed. After waving to someone inside, she walked out and headed straight for him. He rolled down the window.

"Problem?" she asked.

"Won't start," he admitted. "I'll have to radio in for someone to come get it."

"Oh, but we're still going to the police artist, right?" she asked. "You can ride with me."

"I can't just leave the car here. I'll have to turn over the keys, sign papers—"

"Jillian, my office manager, can hold the keys for you and give them to whomever. She's bonded and insured. For that matter, Fritzie, one of my drivers, is a great mechanic. You should let her take a look at that engine."

Michael wasn't about to turn over his car keys to the associate of a suspected felon. That was strictly against policy. But if he didn't get Wendy to the police artist now, while she had enthusiasm, he might lose the opportunity.

He climbed out of the car and pocketed the keys, then grabbed his cellular phone. He'd deal with the car later. "Let's just go," he said.

Wendy looked relieved as they both climbed back into her van. It wasn't until they were well on the road that she sprang the news that she had to make a couple of "quick stops" on the way downtown.

"I allocated as many tasks as I could to my staff," she explained, "but Bobbie's still out with the flu, and a couple of my customers won't let anyone but me handle their business. Then there's Yoda."

"Yoda?"

"You'll see," she said with an enigmatic smile that caused his objections to die a-birthing. She was breathtaking when she smiled, which wasn't all that often, at least not in his presence. Then again, he hadn't given her much to smile about.

He kept silent during the trip to the dry cleaner's to pick up some senator's daughter's clothes and deliver them to her town house. The stop at an art gallery where they restored paintings was educational. How did Wendy make such contacts, anyway? And had they come across any of the material stolen from the Art Deco Museum?

They stopped at Eatzi's, a gourmet restaurant/grocery store, for pistachio nuts, sirloin tips, and a cheesecake ready for the table. Wendy seemed to know everyone, and she whizzed in and out with unbelievable efficiency.

"Put it on my tab," she called over her shoulder to one of the white-aproned employees as she walked out without paying. As she stored everything in specially designed compartments in the back of her van, which prevented fragile items from rolling around and smushing or breaking, she explained, "It's much easier to shop at places where I have an arrangement like that. Standing in line to pay wastes loads of time."

The gourmet comestibles were delivered to the apartment of some yuppie, out to impress his date for that evening. Michael wondered if he'd ever been that young or that eager to please a woman. He didn't think so. He used to barbecue hamburgers for Faye out on the patio and open a bottle of Chianti. That was about as fancy as it got.

On the way to the next stop, his curiosity overcame him. "This is a helluva strange way to make a living," he said. "How did you get into it?"

She smiled. He imagined she heard that question a lot.

"I didn't set out to become a personal shopper," she explained. "It just sort of evolved. The truth of the matter is, I love to shop. I can't pass up a white sale. I read the inserts of the newspaper the way a financial analyst reads the stock quotes. My favorite place in the whole wide world is a shopping mall the day after Thanksgiving."

Michael's blood ran cold. Wendy's enthusiasm was just a little too reminiscent of Faye's for his comfort.

"And money's like a river, right?" he couldn't help commenting. "You just dip in and take whatever you need for whatever you want, 'cause there's lots more coming down the pike." That was how Faye had described it to him during one of the rare instances she had admitted she had a problem.

But Wendy looked appalled at his suggestion.

"Heavens, no. My clients usually put me on a strict budget. One of the lures of hiring a personal shopper is that you can actually save money because I hunt down the bargains you don't have time to find."

That was a revelation to him. "So these rich people you shop for actually pay attention to how much you spend?"

"You bet. For each client, I have to render an accounting down to the penny, complete with receipts."

That practice would have been alien to Faye, Michael admitted silently. She used to have clothes, shoes, and purses delivered to the office where she worked part-time as a secretary, so that he wouldn't know how much she actually spent. She never remembered to record checks in the register, so they were continually overdrawing the account no matter how much money he put into it. She hid the credit card bills from him or "lost" them.

"How long have you been in business?" he asked.

"Officially five years. But I did it unofficially for years, starting when I was in high school. I went to Hockaday—you know about Hockaday?"

He knew. Hockaday was a private girls' school in North Dallas. Only the richest of the rich sent their kids there. But Hockaday was no fluffy finishing school. Academically it could compete with any prep school in the country.

"I'm familiar with the school," he said.

"I went there 'cause I could play a mean game of tennis," she admitted. "I wasn't one of those brainy kids, though I wished I could have been. Straight A's could have gotten me a scholarship to college as well. Tennis got me some nifty trophies and ribbons, and an elbow that still swells up in cold weather."

"You didn't go to college?"

"Just junior college. A couple of years. I thought I wanted to go into fashion merchandising, but I couldn't afford any of the colleges that offered those kinds of programs."

Couldn't afford? Those were words he hadn't expected to hear from a shopping addict. Certainly they'd never passed Faye's lips. Faye's rich parents had never denied her anything. It just simply never occurred to her that something she wanted to buy didn't fit into the budget. "I thought you grew up rich," he said.

"Far from it, I'm afraid." She stopped for a red light. "I went to high school on a scholarship. My father . . ." Her voice trailed off as she leaned to look at herself in the rearview mirror. "My father died when I was three. My mom had to struggle. She had me clipping coupons from the time I was in kindergarten."

"But what about tennis?" Michael persisted. "I always thought of tennis as a rich person's sport."

"I learned at the local rec center. My school gym teacher coached me for free, and I played at the city park. Hockaday had an aggressive tennis program. A coach from there saw me at the park one day. That's how I got the scholarship. It seemed like a real blessing at the time."

"Seemed like?" Michael asked.

"It's not easy being the only poor girl at a rich girls' school." A shadow crossed her face, a memory of the adolescent pain of not belonging, Michael imagined. "But I compensated."

"How?"

"I didn't have much money, but I had taste galore. I would organize a group shopping expedition and help all the girls pick out new wardrobes. I got the vicarious pleasure of spending money on quality merchandise, my newfound friends got makeovers, and pretty soon every girl in the school wanted me to help her buy her clothes."

"And you started charging a fee," Michael concluded, thinking that her approach was pretty clever.

"Not right away. At first my only motivation was to be popular." She blushed, turning her cheeks a lovely peachy-pink color that Michael found more than charming.

He'd never seen that kind of guilelessness in a grown woman. He felt a strong urge to kiss her, especially when she looked over at him through the veil of her long eyelashes, seeming to expect some reaction.

"All kids want to belong," he said, hoping she would continue. "When did you start charging for your services?"

"Only after I was in college and I really needed the money. I read in a magazine about a personal shopper in New York, and I thought, 'I could do that!' It was an epiphany. My old high school friends were my first clients."

She paused and took a sip of coffee from the foam

cup he'd purchased earlier for her. He imagined it must be stone cold. "Did you actually make money?" he asked.

"A little. Through word of mouth the business grew pretty quickly. I incorporated the Born to Shop name five years ago and expanded into running errands, meal planning, party planning. I started advertising on cable TV about six months ago, and I immediately had to hire three new people. Now the company is almost bigger than I can handle, and it's actually supporting me."

That explained her sudden prosperity, Michael thought, adjusting his thinking moment by moment. That would teach him to nurse preconceived notions. If this background spiel she'd just given him was true, why would she be tempted to trade stolen merchandise?

Granted, her business gave her a great front. She could easily manufacture a believable cover story for being in any part of town or talking to just about anyone. But if her business was finally taking off, why would she risk everything by fencing stolen merchandise?

She could have huge debts, he reminded himself. His investigation into her finances had only begun.

Wendy pulled the van into a parking lot of an old warehouse just east of downtown. The warehouse, once a paper bag factory, had been converted into posh apartments. After finding a spot to park, Wendy pulled out her electronic organizer, consulted some file, then riffled through her huge key ring until she located a particular key. All of the keys had stickers with numbers printed on them.

She acknowledged his curious look with an explanation. "I don't put clients' names on their keys, in case the key ring should ever be lost or stolen," she said. "So I number them all. The file with the numbers and corresponding names is in my organizer, protected by a password so that if *it's* ever lost or stolen, none of the proprietary information can be accessed. I have clients' credit card numbers, alarm codes, all sorts of things stored in here."

She tapped the little black mini-computer, then tucked it into a pocket of her denim vest.

She was unbearably clever and efficient, he decided right then and there. "Do you ever take a breath?" he asked impulsively.

THREE

Wendy looked at Michael, blinked her big green eyes owlishly, then narrowed them. "Well. If I was talking too much, why didn't you say so?" She opened the door and hopped out of the van.

He followed quickly. *Way to go, Tagg,* he congratulated himself. His job was to keep Wendy talking. That was how people incriminated themselves. Most suspects clammed up in the presence of a detective, because they knew the less said, the fewer lies they would have to weave. Now, when for once in his life he had a chatty suspect, he managed to insult her and probably shut her up for good.

"You weren't talking too much," he said when he'd caught up with her. In truth, he'd enjoyed her story a lot. Entrepreneurs had always fascinated him. He enjoyed his work, but he couldn't imagine how anyone stayed motivated without a time clock to punch and a regular paycheck to look forward to. "I didn't mean that at all. I was in awe of your efficiency, all the work you accomplish in the same twenty-four hours the rest of us have. I was wondering how you have time to breathe, much less eat and sleep."

She hardly looked mollified as she punched in a security code at the warehouse's front entrance. Her pretty pink lips, which were naturally pouty, were now pressed into a firm line of grim determination.

"I just wonder if you're ever, you know, lazy," Michael continued, trying to bail himself out of hot water. "Do you ever sit around and eat too much pizza? Do you ever channel surf? Do you ever linger over coffee at breakfast, reading the paper?"

She still didn't respond, but she looked as if she might be thinking about it. The door buzzed, admitting them to the building's cool interior. "I guess I don't like to sit in one place too long," she finally said. "Some people have referred to me as manic, but I like to think of myself as energetic. I have a TV, but I haven't turned it on since Wimbledon last year. I like pizza, but it's so high in fat, I try to limit myself to one slice at a time. As for lingering over coffee, not usually. Most mornings I brew it while I'm in the shower, dump it into a travel mug, and drink it on the way to work."

"Not usually." He followed her into the starkly decorated building, feeling a grudging admiration for the way she'd neatly put him in his place. "But every once in a while?"

She punched the elevator Up button, then glanced over at him. A mischievous smile took over her face.

"Sunday mornings. Sunday mornings are mine and mine alone, and I linger."

The elevator doors opened and she stepped inside, leaving him standing stock-still for a moment, his overactive imagination building all sorts of pictures. The way she'd said the word *linger*, stretching out to four syllables, made him wonder, What exactly did she mean? He pictured her lounging on the sofa in a teddy, drinking cappuccino and leafing through a lingerie catalog.

"Are you coming?" she asked impatiently.

He practically jumped into the elevator, trying to bring his bodily reactions under control before he embarrassed himself.

Wendy was appalled at what she'd just done. She had actually flirted with the odious Detective Michael Taggert! She hadn't set out to do it. But his acute interest in her background, her business, was flattering. He was a fantastic listener. And given that she was a gifted talker, a good listener was a rare treasure.

She realized now he hadn't meant to insult her, and she wished she hadn't been so quick to jump to conclusions. That was why she'd offered him a mild flirtation, she decided. To prove to him that all was forgiven.

But it wasn't, she reminded herself. He'd horribly disrupted her life with his shoddy investigation, and it would be a cold day in hell before she forgave him anything. She'd better keep her mind firmly on her priorities—namely, tracking down Mr. Neff and finding out what was really going on.

She found Mr. Damian's apartment, knocked to make sure no one was home, then unlocked the dead bolt with her key. She didn't open the door all the way, however. She pushed it open only a crack. "Yoda? Where are you, puppy?"

A low, menacing growl issued from inside the apartment.

"It's me, Wendy, remember? I'm the one who gives you yummy treats." She pulled an extra-large-sized Milkbone from her skirt pocket and pushed it through the crack.

The growling stopped, replaced by snuffling and crunching.

"Good Lord, what's in there?" Michael asked. "Sounds like one of those brontosauruses from *Jurassic Park*."

"It's Yoda. He's a rottweiler with a self-esteem problem. He thinks he's not lovable, so he hates everyone first before they can hate him."

"You're a pet psychologist too?"

"I'm just repeating what his owner told me." She opened the door wide enough to reveal Yoda's big black face. His ears were perked, and he looked up at Wendy hopefully. She could see that his nub of a tail was wagging. "Good boy."

The rottweiler allowed her to enter the apartment without a whimper of protest. But when Michael started to follow, the dog whirled, bristled, and growled, challenging.

"I'll just wait out here," Michael said, retreating to the safety of the hallway.

Wendy stifled her laughter. "Ooooh, big brave cop. You're not afraid to slap handcuffs on a five-foot-two woman, but you back off quick at a real threat."

"Five-foot-two women don't bite," he pointed out. "At least, not usually."

"Are you sure?" She was doing it again. Flirting. She had to stop. This man was not her friend! If he got the idea she was coming on to him, he would think she was trying to seduce him so he would use his influence to get the charges against her dropped.

Jeez, if she thought it would work, she might try it. Given a choice between prison and a night of passionate lovemaking with Mr. Law-and-Order . . . Hmm. She'd best not even go there. She'd already determined he didn't need to get his kicks through nefarious channels.

She quickly located Yoda's leash and collar. He poked his head through the choke chain, eager for his walk.

"You okay in there?" Michael called. "Still have all your appendages?"

"Yoda's a pussycat once you get to know him." She came back to the door with an enthusiastic Yoda in tow. Once they were out in the hallway, Yoda no longer considered Michael a threat. While Wendy locked the door, the dog sniffed Michael, thigh to ankle on both legs, then licked his hand.

"Hey, you're not such a brute after all, are you, buddy?" Michael crouched down and scratched the dog behind his ears. Yoda licked Michael on the face, and Michael let him do it.

Somehow the sight of the big bad cop sharing a moment of male bonding with Yoda gave Wendy a catch in her throat. She never imagined Michael could have a softer side, or that he would even like dogs.

"How far do you have to walk this beast, anyway?" he asked, straightening.

"For about fifteen or twenty minutes. There's a little park down the street. We usually go there."

"You know, you could have warned me your little 'stops' were going to add over an hour to our trip downtown."

"An hour? Really?"

"Don't play dumb," he scoffed. "You know down to the second how long each errand takes. I've seen you making notations in your organizer."

He'd caught her there. "Yeah, okay. I guess I knew I was pushing your goodwill. But you could have objected earlier. I really need to take care of these tasks, and I didn't think the delay was bothering you too much, especially since you were sort of interrogating me along the way."

He laughed. "That wasn't an interrogation, and you know it. That was raw curiosity about what makes you tick. I thought you were exactly like my ex-wife. But you're not, thank God."

She tried to picture him with a wife. The image wouldn't come into focus. She couldn't imagine him in a state of domestic bliss. "You were married?" she blurted out, curious herself.

"Eight long years. Faye was a semiprofessional shopper."

She had no idea what he was talking about. "Semiprofessional?"

"Yeah. Like you, she loved to shop and she loved to spend other people's money. Unfortunately, she only bought things for herself, and she spent all of *my* money plus a lot I didn't have."

Ah. A lot of things fell into place. No wonder he'd been so hostile to her at first. Not only did he believe she was a felon, but he thought she had a despicable vocation as well.

Even as an unwelcome tendril of envy wound its way into her psyche, Wendy found herself wanting to defend the hapless Faye. "She must have had other qualities that compensated."

"She was always well dressed," Michael said dismissively. "Sorry I can't be more charitable, but I've spent the last seven years paying off the debts she incurred—fifty-four thousand dollars' worth."

"Ouch." Wendy no longer felt like defending the woman. As much as she loved nice things, she was excruciatingly responsible with her own meager funds. Although she used credit cards for everything, she always paid her bills in full when they arrived.

Michael grew silent as they walked the three blocks toward the park. Wendy noticed that he paused often, surreptitiously glancing behind them.

"Don't look now," he said, "but there's a brown Caprice behind us. It circled the block once already."

"It's probably only someone looking for a parking

place," she said, unconcerned. "Parking is hard to come by in this neighborhood. You really are a suspicious type, aren't you?"

"It's my job to be suspicious."

They walked on in surprisingly companionable silence until they reached the park. Well, "park" was stretching it some. A patch of grass, a couple of scraggly trees, and a peeling bench was the best that could be managed in this concrete-bound part of town.

"I'm going to run with Yoda a little ways," she said. "You can run with me if you want, or wait for me here." She nodded toward the park bench.

He looked down at his lizard boots. "I'm not exactly dressed for jogging, so I'll wait here. Don't leave my sight, though," he cautioned. "I don't like the looks of this neighborhood, and that car bothers me."

She looked around. The brown car was nowhere in sight. Still, the idea that someone might be stalking her gave her an unpleasant shiver. More than once in her life she'd been the victim of persistent, unwanted advances from men.

"I plan to stay right here in the park," she said. "But really, who would mess with me when I've got this beast attached to me?" She gave Yoda a pat before starting off at an easy jog. Yoda broke into a trot and quickly outpaced her, straining on the leash.

She picked up her speed, feeling a bit awkward running in her sandals and miniskirt. She wished she'd chosen to wear a warm-up suit today, but the beautiful spring weather and her sense of blessed freedom had dictated the denim outfit.

Still, stretching her muscles felt good. She'd been too busy to jog lately. She would have enjoyed the exercise more if she hadn't been worried about Michael watching her, and whether she looked silly.

Everything was going fine until a squirrel darted out of a tree practically under Yoda's nose. He gave a snort and bolted. Unprepared, Wendy couldn't hold on to the leash, although she made a valiant effort. The dog's sudden surge forward jerked her off her feet and onto her chest, dragging her a couple of feet before she let go with a cry of anguish.

Michael was there in an instant. He'd been all the way across the park—he must have flown to her side.

"Wendy, are you all right?" he demanded sharply, though his hands were gentle as he helped her up. "Easy. Nothing broken?"

"Never mind me," she said urgently. "Go after the dog. I'll be in big trouble if anything happens to Yoda." Dismissing her minor scrapes and bruises, she took off after the rottweiller, which had gained a considerable lead on her. He darted across the street, barely missing a collision with a passing car, and galloped into a parking lot.

Wendy put on a burst of speed, her only thought to catch Yoda before he got lost or injured. Mr. Damian loved that dog the way he would his own child. She would never forgive herself if something happened to the animal. Mr. Damian trusted her and no one else to exercise his rotty.

She started to leap off the curb into the street when a strong pair of hands grabbed her, knocking her off balance. For the second time in two minutes she found herself on the ground not by her own choice. This time Michael Taggert was on top of her.

She was just about to berate him for being some kind of maniac when the hot breath of a passing car whooshed over her. *My God*, she thought, her head spinning, *that car would have hit me!* She'd been so engrossed in catching Yoda that she hadn't been paying attention.

Her second realization, all in the span of a few seconds, was that having Michael's big, hard body on top of hers wasn't such an unpleasant experience. She felt her body responding to him in a purely female way, heating up from the core outward.

"Get off me," she said through clenched teeth, masking her sudden and inappropriate desire with hostility.

Michael was breathing hard, matching her gasp for gasp. He must have been right beside her through the chase, she thought.

"You almost got yourself killed," he finally managed. He didn't move.

She tempered her voice. "I know. I've got to find Yoda. Please get off."

This time he did ease himself away from her. He sprang to his feet and offered her a hand up.

A familiar panting noise caused her to turn and look behind her. There was Yoda, hunkered down on his elbows with his rump in the air, wanting to play.

"So, you think that was funny, do you, Yoda?" she scolded. She placed her hand in Michael's warm grasp and allowed him to pull her to her feet. She grabbed Yoda's leash on the way up. "We're going straight home, now, and you can forget about that second Milkbone you were going to get."

She knew she should say something to Michael. The man had just possibly saved her life. But she couldn't force herself to be grateful. It was easier to focus on the dog.

"You're bleeding," Michael said, pointing to a scrape on her knee. A tiny trickle of blood wended its way down her leg.

She swiped at it impatiently. With all the adrenaline in her system, she didn't feel any pain. "It's nothing. Let's just take Yoda home and get on with meeting the artist. I've wasted enough of your time today."

Wendy's sudden ambivalence toward him cast a shadow on Michael's morning. He'd actually been enjoying all the detours. Watching Wendy work was educational, not to mention arousing. Throwing her down to the ground and falling on top of her would have been pretty fun, too, if he hadn't been scared out of his mind. If he'd been even one second later in pulling her out of the street, she would be roadkill.

She didn't seem to realize how close she'd come to meeting her maker. She hadn't even thanked him for saving her from certain injury. Instead she seemed withdrawn and even a little bit angry.

"The car that almost hit you," he said as they walked toward the warehouse building. "Did you realize it was the same brown Caprice that was circling the block?"

"Really? Maybe he was in a hurry 'cause he spotted a parking place."

Michael didn't think so. There'd been something almost deliberate in the way that car had barreled down the street without hesitation, and the driver hadn't even stopped after the near-accident.

In all the confusion, Michael still had managed to memorize part of the license plate. The Caprice was a few years old and not a very common color. He intended to track down the driver and find out what the hell he or she was up to. At the very least, he would turn the person over to the Traffic Division for reckless driving.

Wendy reinstated Yoda in his apartment and, despite her threat, gave him another Milkbone. Minutes later they were back in her van headed for the police department's Physical Evidence Section on Cantegral. Michael tried to get Wendy talking again, but she answered his questions with monosyllables, so he gave up.

Although Michael hadn't made an appointment with the artist, Linda Bashier was almost always available, and today was no exception. They found her in her second-floor cubbyhole of an office, messing around with modeling clay.

The moment Linda and Wendy met, Michael could tell they would get along. Wendy's reticence disappeared as soon as she entered Linda's area. Her natural curiosity rebounded, and she launched a series of endless questions about the artist's work.

"What's this?" she asked, examining a life-size model of the head of a young male, made out of clay.

"It's a facial reconstruction," Linda replied. "A badly decomposed body was found near the Trinity River, and we couldn't identify it. So I take the skull and, using certain standard measurements, build a face of clay around—"

Wendy gasped. "You mean there's a human skull under there?"

Linda shared a wink with Michael. "Yes. I boil it in an acid solution to clean off—"

"Whoa, whoa," Wendy said, holding up her hands in a warding-off gesture. "That's more than I wanted to know."

"Sorry," Linda said. "I forget how repugnant some people find my work. Shall we get busy?"

The two women settled at a desk with a sketch pad and a thick book that contained facial features of every description. Linda would help Wendy remember every detail, then combine them into a drawing, or perhaps a couple of different ones showing the suspect with and without hair, with and without glasses. Michael planned to circulate the drawing among all the cops, snitches, and other criminal elements, hoping someone would recognize the mug.

During the two hours it took to come up with the composite drawing, Michael made a few phone calls and took care of his stranded car. Unfortunately, the motor pool didn't have even a bicycle to spare as a loaner, so he was stuck without wheels. That meant that if he wanted to pal around with Wendy anymore, he would still be the victim of her whims.

The prospect wasn't nearly as unpleasant as it should have been.

He spent the rest of the time on the phone with banks and utility companies, following leads on Neff and the mysterious Pat Walters. The bank, it turned out, did have an account for Bernard Neff. They were tracking down the person who'd taken the original account information.

Unfortunately, the account had been cleaned out through a series of ATM withdrawals over the past several weeks. It sounded as if Wendy's friend had plans. Maybe he'd even set Wendy up to be caught, to clear the way so he could move cleanly on to his next heist.

At least he hadn't gotten those last few thousand dollars from the sale of the art deco jewelry, Michael thought. The cash and the jewels were locked up tight in the evidence room.

Bored, Michael decided to wander over to visit Cecil Wanstadt, the resident fingerprint expert. The shiny surface of the topaz on one of the art deco necklaces had yielded a single, fairly clear print. Wanstadt had quickly determined that it didn't belong to Wendy or to the fence she'd sold the jewelry to. He'd submitted it to the computer fingerprint database to see if a match could be found.

Michael discovered Wanstadt hunched over a keyboard in the room that housed the computer, which the fingerprint expert guarded as if he were a dog with a big bone. On his computer screen were two huge thumbprints, one complete, one partial, which Wanstadt was comparing ridge by ridge.

When calling out Cecil's name yielded no response, Michael had to tap him on the shoulder to get his attention.

Wanstadt jumped, then broke into a big grin. "Hey, Taggert, what are you doing on this side of the tracks?" he asked as he stood and offered a handshake.

"Came to harass you. Any luck with the jewelry print?"

The older man shook his head. "The computer spit out four candidates for comparison, but when I eyeballed 'em, none matched."

Michael felt disappointment settle inside his chest like a lead weight. That was the way this case had gone from the beginning, one dead end after another. Although it was encouraging that Wendy's prints hadn't been found on the jewelry, she was still his only suspect. If something more concrete didn't turn up soon, she was in a heap of trouble, and so was he.

He hoped the mayor was bluffing about nixing Michael's application to the FBI, but what if he wasn't? He figured he had a few more days' grace, but then he would have to prove Wendy's guilt or innocence to get himself off the hook.

"Hey, Tagg, that you in the computer room?" an anonymous voice called from the main squad room.

Michael stuck his head out the doorway. "Someone want me?"

A detective he'd seen often at the courthouse pointed at the phone. "Call for you. Line four."

Michael picked up the extra extension in the computer room. "Taggert here."

"It's me, Joe. I was just talking to Smythe."

Wayne Smythe was another detective in Theft. "Yeah?"

"You're not going to like this."

The lead weight in Michael's chest doubled in size and sank to his gut. "What? Spit it out."

"Four houses burglarized in the last five months were owned by clients of Born to Shop."

FOUR

"It gets worse," Joe said.

Michael braced himself. "Go ahead."

"Whoever committed the burglaries got around the security alarms."

Michael flashed back to Wendy punching in the security code at Yoda's owner's apartment building. "Is there more?"

"Oh, yeah. The diamond earrings we found in Wendy's purse. You know how they weren't part of the estate jewelry stolen from the museum?"

"Yeah?"

"They belong to a Mrs. Howard Pitts."

"One of Wendy's clients," Michael guessed.

"You got it."

This new development shed a really ugly light on Wendy. Yet something didn't feel right about it. It was too neat. Surely if Wendy were routinely ripping off her clients, she would fake a forced entry, maybe set off the alarm on her way out the door with the loot. Otherwise she would have to know she was implicating herself.

"Thanks, Joe." Thanks for making a bad day worse.

"Smythe wants to bring her in for another interrogation."

Now Michael's insides felt like solid lead, no more room for expansion. Poor Wendy. He'd never sided with a perp, even a possible perp, before. Still, he didn't relish the thought of the wringer his coworker, Wayne Smythe, would put her through. That guy could make hardened felons, gang members, and ex-cons cry. "Let me see if I can get her to come in voluntarily, okay? She's already in the system. No need for handcuffs and warrants."

Joe laughed. "You're getting soft, Tagg."

Michael didn't rise to the bait. "Maybe so."

He got a few more details from Joe before he ended the call. Just as he hung up, he became pleasantly aware of a fragrance he was coming to know: Wendy. He turned, and she was standing by the door in the computer room.

"I'm done," she said. Her eyes sparkled with enthusiasm. "Wait till you see what Linda came up with. It looks exactly like Mr. Neff."

Michael had a hard time coming up with a pleasant rejoinder. He had a sudden visual image of Wendy in prison blues. Maybe that shark lawyer of hers could work out a deal, especially if the mayor remained on Wendy's side. But with this new evidence that had come to light, even the mayor would have a hard time believing in Wendy's innocence.

Then why was Michael so anxious to believe there was an alternative explanation?

"Michael?" Wendy looked at him questioningly. "Don't you want to see it? Linda's putting the finishing touches on it now."

"She'll fax it over to me when she's done, I'm sure," Michael said curtly.

"Is something wrong? You look . . . funny."

"Yeah, something's real wrong." He consulted his notebook. "Hopkins. Lamb. Pitts. Yarbrough. Names sound familiar?"

Wendy paled. "They're all clients of mine. Why?"

"They've all been burglarized in the last few months."

"Oh, Mrs. Lamb said something to me about that. They took her silver, her furs. But I hadn't realized there was a rash of—wait a minute! You think I had something to do with it?"

At her shrill question several heads turned. Wendy, bristling with outrage, ignored them.

"What I think is immaterial. Detective Wayne Smythe wants to talk to you."

Wendy's head was spinning as they walked outside the Physical Evidence building into the warm, pleasant spring day. Things were going from bad to worse! Her spirits had been momentarily bolstered by the super-accurate drawing she and the artist had produced. But for every step forward she took, it seemed she took two steps back.

Now the police thought she was a museum thief *and* a second-story woman.

The very idea that she would victimize the lovely people who brought her business, who trusted her with so many very important responsibilities, who made possible the life she wanted to lead—she was nauseated at the thought.

"Do you keep a calendar?" Michael asked. It was the first thing he'd said since they'd climbed into her van five minutes earlier.

"Yes. Why?"

"Do you have it with you?"

"It's in my organizer."

"Bring it in with you to the station. They'll want to know what you were doing, specifically, on the days the burglaries occurred. If you were out of town, or spending the night with . . ." He paused. "Well, you know. If someone can vouch for you, and you can establish an alibi, it'll help. A lot."

Wendy's face warmed at the mention of "spending the night." It was not something she was particularly proud of, but if James could provide her with an alibi, she'd kiss him *and* his new girlfriend.

"I haven't been out of town much, but I do know someone who can verify that I don't go gallivanting out to break into houses in the middle of the night."

"Who?" Michael barked.

If Wendy hadn't known better, she'd believe there was a jealous note in his question.

"James. James Batliner."

"You have a boyfriend?"

"You sound really surprised."

"It's just that . . . you never mentioned a guy in your life."

"That's because he's actually my ex-boyfriend," Wendy said, matching Michael's snappish tone. "He dumped me yesterday, and I've been trying to block him from my mind."

"You don't sound terribly broken up about it."

"I saw it coming, so it wasn't a big surprise. He was cheating on me. But I'm sure he'll provide me an alibi if he can."

"Did you spend a lot of nights with him?"

She cocked her head and gave Michael a sideways glance. "Is this an official question, or are you just being nosy?"

He didn't even crack a smile. "I just figured if you were with him most nights, your chances of providing an alibi are higher."

Wendy still wasn't sure she should answer. She realized then that she was a little embarrassed about her relationship with James. They hadn't exactly been in love, yet she'd spent a couple of nights at his house.

Deep down, Wendy knew she'd slept with James because he was a nice, likable guy she felt at ease around. Well, she used to think that, anyway.

But she was better than that. Loneliness was no excuse for holding on to a less-than-fulfilling relationship.

"There's a good chance James can alibi me on at

least one of the nights the burglaries occurred," she said carefully.

"How did you know the burglaries occurred at night?" Michael asked casually.

Damn, he thought she was guiltier than ever. She'd believed that maybe, now that they'd gotten to know each other a little better, he would have realized she wasn't capable of a life of crime.

"Don't most break-ins occur at night?" she shot back.

"A lot of burglaries take place during the day, when the residents are at work."

"Well, *did* these occur at night?"

"Yeah. In all four cases, the homeowners were out of town. That's information you would be privy to."

Lord, no wonder they thought she'd done it. Someone had carried out a damn professional job framing her, and she had a pretty good idea who.

"What about the people in your office?" Michael asked hopefully. "Do any of them have access to the schedules and security access codes?"

"Jillian, my office manager. But there's no way she would be involved in anything like that. I've known her for years."

"Does anyone else have access to your organizer?" Michael asked.

Wendy gasped. "That's it! Mr. Neff was curious about it one day, so I showed him how it worked. He didn't seem to really understand it—you know how most old people are about computers. But he could have been faking it."

"Did he ever have the opportunity to pull information from it? What about the password?"

Wendy deflated. "That's right, the password. There's no way he could have had access to that information." The names of her clients he could have gotten from other sources, but the security codes were a different matter.

"Think, Wendy. How could a third party get hold of those security codes?"

"I don't know," she said miserably. "I keep a backup of my organizer files on my computers at home and at the office, but no one has access to that, either. I guess someone could follow me around and use binoculars to watch me punching in security codes." She thought again of the car that had almost run her down.

She wanted to dismiss it as coincidence, a stroke of almost-bad luck. But maybe the guy in the brown Caprice *had* been following her.

"That's not a bad theory," Michael said. "I know long-distance access codes have been stolen that way. Bring it up during your questioning. Anything you can inject to stir up doubt will help."

Was Michael Taggert coaching her on how to get through an interrogation? Interesting. He'd gone from browbeating, sneering bad cop to cheerleader good cop in less than twenty-four hours. The change was welcome, but she didn't entirely trust it—or him.

Her car phone rang. What now? She punched the button for the no-hands speaker phone. "Wendy Thayer."

"Wendy, I'm so glad I caught you!" It was Jillian, her office manager. "Maggie Courtland just called. She has an appointment with her doctor, and her car won't start. Can you take her?"

"A lot of that going around," Michael murmured.

"For heaven's sake, why doesn't she call a cab?" Wendy asked.

"I asked her the same thing, but she doesn't like cabs. She had a bad experience once with a driver who took her out into the boonies and mugged her."

"Oh." Wendy could understand the woman's reticence. She'd encountered a scary cab driver or two in her time.

"She's on the other line," Jillian said. "Please, can I tell her you'll come get her? She sounds desperate, and you know she's about ten months pregnant."

"Can't someone else do it?" Wendy asked, a little desperation creeping into her voice. She would have to level with Jillian eventually, but she didn't want to do it now, with Michael listening in.

"Everyone else is frantic and running late, what with all the extra errands you stuck on everybody this morning. You don't have to wait for Maggie at the doctor's or anything."

Wendy put Jillian on hold and looked over at Michael. "Would you mind? Mrs. Courtland lives right off Oak Lawn near Brighton. It's only about ten minutes away."

Michael rolled his eyes. "The day is shot anyway. Sure, why not?"

"Great." Wendy confirmed with Jillian that she was on the way, then hung up.

Maggie Courtland lived in a huge house—a mansion, really—on wooded, hilly St. Johns Street. Michael gave a low whistle as Wendy pulled into the driveway. "I'm surprised this Mrs. Courtland doesn't have a chauffeur-driven limo."

"Actually she does," Wendy said. "But the driver keeps pretty busy shuttling Maggie's husband around."

Wendy didn't even have to honk or go to the door. Mrs. Courtland was waiting. Pretty, blond, and about Wendy's age, she scurried out the door and duck-walked toward the waiting van amazingly fast for a woman who looked as if she'd swallowed a watermelon.

"Good Lord, she looks like she should have had the kid last month," Michael said under his breath before hopping out of the van to help the woman into the back seat.

"Would you be more comfortable in front?" he asked when Maggie was halfway in.

"Oh, no, I like it back here. I can stretch out a bit." She sounded out of breath, and her face was pale. "Wendy, hi. Who's your friend?"

"New employee," Wendy answered before Michael could tell her the truth. "I'm training him. You're due in a couple of weeks, aren't you?" she asked as Maggie got situated and Michael took his seat in front.

"Yes, mid-April. But I think the doc got the due

date wrong. This is my fourth baby, and I've learned to tell . . . well, there are signs, you know?"

"Mm," Wendy said noncommittally. She knew next to nothing about having babies. "Where's your doctor?"

"In Preston Center. On Luther and—oh!"

"Luther and what?" Wendy asked as she pulled out of the driveway.

"Luther and—omigod!

Omigod? She'd never heard of that street.

"Uh, Wendy, I think we have a problem," Michael said. He didn't raise his voice, but there was a definite note of panic there.

Wendy stopped the van and turned to look at her back-seat passenger. Maggie's face was contorted with pain, and she clutched her swollen belly. "Maggie, what's wrong?"

"What do you think's wrong?" Michael asked, unfastening his seat belt. "The woman's in labor."

Maggie took a few gasping breaths. "Your friend's right. My water just broke. Better skip the doctor and head straight for the hospital."

Wendy's hands started shaking. She'd had some odd experiences as a personal shopper, but she'd never delivered a pregnant woman to the hospital before. "Which hospital?"

"Presbyterian," Maggie answered. "Please, hurry. My babies come quick, and this one feels impatient—oh!"

"Take Central," Michael ordered. "On second thought, I'll drive. You take care of Mrs. Courtland."

He had such authority in his voice that Wendy didn't offer any argument. She threw the van into Park, unfastened her seat belt, and climbed into the back.

Michael scooted behind the wheel, shifted the seat back, and had the van in motion in seconds flat.

"Don't take Central Expressway," Wendy said as she helped Maggie lie down on the back seat, using a wadded-up denim jacket as a pillow. "The construction is murder. Take Oak Lawn to Walnut Hill."

"Too many lights and school zones," Michael argued. "This time of day there won't be much traffic on the freeway. It'll be faster."

"There's always traffic!"

Maggie, in the throes of another contraction, gave a strangled cry.

"Michael, she's having another contraction!" Wendy said. "She just had one."

Maggie gripped Wendy's arm. "It'll be all right, Wendy," she said, though her eyes were a little wild. "My babies always pop out without any problem. I've got good hips, my doctor says."

"You're not reassuring me. I can't deliver a baby, Maggie. So just hold it in till we get to the hospital."

Maggie shook her head. "It doesn't work that way, friend. I didn't want to tell you, but I've been having contractions for over an hour." Her face contorted in pain, and when the contraction released her, she actually screamed. "Wendy! The baby's coming. He's not fooling around. Help me get my clothes off."

Fighting off hysteria, Wendy did as Maggie instructed.

"You're having it right now?" Michael asked.

"Yes," Maggie replied, panting now. "We should find, you know, something to wrap him in when he gets here."

"Newspaper!" Wendy said. "I saw that in a movie once. Newspapers are sanitary." She leaned over the back seat and rooted around until she found the paper she'd picked up from her porch that morning and tossed in back, unread. There it was, still rolled into its pink plastic bag.

She was vaguely aware of the van turning onto the Central Expressway access road. "Don't get on Central," she said to Michael again, but he didn't listen. Why did men always think they were smarter when it came to driving? She spent eight hours a day in her car running all over town. She *knew* what routes were faster.

"Look, see? Almost no traffic."

Wendy raised up and looked out the windshield. The lanes ahead did look pretty clear, until they came over the first rise. "What's that?"

"What?" Michael asked.

"That sign. It says the road's narrowing down to one lane."

"It doesn't matter," Maggie said, sounding a little calmer now. "I wouldn't have made it anyway. I need to push."

"No!" Wendy and Michael said together. Michael added, "Five minutes, tops, and we'll be at the hospital." Even as those words were leaving his lips, he had to put on the brakes. After thirty seconds of creeping bumper to bumper, they came to a dead stop.

"We're not moving," Wendy pointed out.

"They're moving a big crane in the road up ahead. We're not going anywhere for a while."

Twenty minutes later they were still stuck in traffic.

"I'm pushing," Maggie said. "You can't stop me."

"Oooh, Michael, the baby's coming," Wendy said, near panic. She could see the crown of its head. "Help me! Please?"

Michael set the brake and unfastened his seat belt, then squeezed between the front seats to join the two women. "Tell me what to do."

"I'm the one who needs help," Maggie groused. "Who's doing all the work here? Help me sit up. Birthing is easier—oh, Lord have mercy—sitting up."

Michael immediately grasped Maggie's shoulders and pulled her up, then slid onto the seat behind her so she could rest against him. "Like that?"

"That's good."

"Maggie, I don't know what to do!" Wendy complained, willing herself not to fall apart. But it turned out she really didn't need help. The baby practically flew into her waiting hands.

Maggie let out an exultant cry. "There! You did it!"

"I didn't do anything!" Wendy objected, holding the tiny scrap of humanity in her hands as if it were a space alien. "You did it all. Michael! I've got a baby here!"

She looked up at her partner in crime. Beaming like an idiot, he was no help at all. "Looks like you're doing just fine," he said. "Is it a girl or a boy?"

Wendy'd been so panicked she forgot to look. She did now. "Oh, it's another boy, Maggie." Her voice trembled with emotion. She'd never seen a baby born except on a film in high school sex education class, and then she'd closed her eyes. "Now you have two of each. Aren't I supposed to hold him upside down or whack him on the butt or something?"

In response, the baby spit something out of his mouth and started wailing.

"You're not expecting me to cut the cord, are you?" she asked Maggie.

"Just put him on my stomach," Maggie said, laughing and crying at the same time. She reached for her new son. "I think the cord can wait for the doctor."

Wendy was only too happy to surrender the baby. She'd gotten so excited during the birth that she'd forgotten about the newspaper. Too late now, she supposed. As she watched Maggie cradling the infant against her stomach, looking for all the world like a Madonna, an intense wave of feelings washed over Wendy. It was the most beautiful thing she'd ever seen.

She wasn't normally the sappy sort, but all at once she started crying.

"Wendy?" Michael asked. "You okay?" He reached out and touched her hair very tentatively.

"F-fine," she said, mortified. That's when she noticed the horns honking. "The traffic's moving again."

Five minutes later they pulled up to the emergency entrance at Presbyterian. Maggie and her baby were whisked away. Wendy, in a daze, left Michael sitting behind the wheel of the van and dashed inside after the gurney, feeling a protectiveness for the mother and baby that was one of the strongest emotions she'd ever experienced.

When it became clear that Wendy wasn't needed anymore, that Maggie was in capable hands, she felt deflated and dazed. A nurse stopped her in the hallway and asked her if she needed help.

"No, I'm fine," she said, even as she looked down at herself and realized she was covered with blood. She ducked into a rest room and cleaned up the best she could. That was when the exultation of witnessing a birth, of being part of it, receded and doubts assailed her.

What if she'd done it all wrong? Maybe she should have used the newspaper after all. Was the baby all right? Was Maggie all right?

As she exited the ladies' room, intent on finding a doctor and getting some answers, she nearly ran over Michael.

"There you are," he said, steadying her with a warm hand to her arm. "You disappeared. I was worried about you."

"Did you think I was fleeing custody?" she asked, only half kidding. She never knew with Michael.

But he was looking at her with an expression she'd

never seen on him before, maybe not on anyone. It was sort of the way someone might look at an angel, or some other miraculous phenomenon.

"You are awesome, Wendy Thayer."

She realized then that he hadn't let go of her arm. "What are you talking about? I was a blundering idiot. I panicked. Thank God I didn't really need to *do* anything."

"You did great," he insisted. Then he looked down at his shoes. "Despite my driving. I should've listened to you and taken Oak Lawn. I appreciate that you didn't say 'I told you so' when the traffic started stacking up."

She would have, she realized, if she hadn't been in such a state of hysterics. She'd missed a perfectly good chance to score a point with her nemesis.

She was about to remedy that situation when something in his eyes stopped her. He was staring at her with this dopey smile gripping his mouth. Then the smile disappeared. Her heart quickened as his face drew closer to hers. He was going to kiss her, she realized. A well of excitement overflowed inside her even as alarm bells sounded between her ears.

"You the one who delivered the baby?"

Michael jerked back as a doctor approached, looking at Wendy.

Wendy nodded and tried to compose herself. Michael had almost kissed her! That was insane. He was still her enemy, even if he had shown himself to be a bit more human.

"That would be me," she said to the doctor.

"Mrs. Courtland is doing fine. The pediatrician is checking over the baby now, but he looked perfectly normal. Seven and a half pounds' worth of healthy boy, with good lungs."

Wendy sagged with relief. "Thank God," she murmured. "I was afraid I'd done something wrong."

"On the contrary, you did a great job. You can see her now. They'll be transferring her to the maternity ward soon, but for now she's still in Treatment Room Five."

Wendy wasted no time hustling to find Maggie. She didn't look at Michael or in any way acknowledge what had almost transpired between them. She hoped they could simply pretend it hadn't happened.

Michael mentally kicked himself six ways to Sunday while they paid their respects to Maggie Courtland, who was beaming from her gurney in the ER.

What had come over him? He would be the first to admit that watching a child being born was a life-altering experience. His throat had felt thick and his eyes had stung when he'd watched Wendy guide that tiny new life into the world.

She claimed she'd done nothing extraordinary, but he knew better. He'd seen the look on her face.

Still, was that any excuse to kiss the woman? Thank God that doctor had come along and interrupted them, or he would have crossed an ethical line from which there was no turning back. Wendy was a suspect in an ongoing investigation—*his* investigation.

Any personal involvement with her would compromise the whole case.

"My husband's on his way," Maggie was saying. "You don't need to stay here and keep me company. I know you have more shopping and errands to do. Jillian said you were swamped."

Actually, Michael thought, the only thing they had pressing was a visit to an interrogation room downtown. If there was any way he could delay that meeting, he would. Wendy could no doubt use a little breathing space.

"If you're sure," Wendy was saying. "I am a little behind schedule."

"Oh, I should pay you." Maggie looked around for her purse. "And I'll pay to have your van cleaned. Your back seat may never be the same."

"That can wait," Wendy assured her with a laugh. "I'll send you a bill. And I promise I won't charge anywhere near what your obstetrician would have."

They said good-bye and had almost cleared Maggie's room when a nurse arrived with a squirming bundle in her arms. "I have your son, Mrs. Courtland," she said.

Michael didn't think he could take any more. He'd never thought much about babies before. Faye had made it clear she didn't want any, and that had suited him fine. He worked too many long hours to be a good father.

Suddenly those long-held convictions were just so much sawdust. This baby was special. The memory of bringing him into the world would be with him for a long time to come. And the memory of Wendy holding him, looking at him with something akin to love even though he was a stranger, would be branded into his memory for life.

He slipped out of the treatment room and left Wendy, Maggie, and the baby to finish up their goodbyes.

FIVE

Wendy was grateful that Michael allowed her to make a detour to her house to change clothes before returning to the police station for more questioning. Funny, but a couple of hours earlier her new status as a burglary suspect had seemed a near mortal blow to her life. Now, after helping a new life come into the world and avoiding the myriad disasters that could have befallen them, she'd put things into perspective.

She would weather this thing just fine, she resolved as she hastily stripped down to her underthings, acutely aware of Michael waiting in her living room with a thin wall separating them. She would answer the questions put to her as completely and honestly as she could, and the truth would set her free.

Or maybe an alibi would. Thank heavens she kept such a detailed calendar.

She dithered only a moment about what to wear. Something conservative, she decided, snatching from her closet a pair of khaki slacks and a modest cotton blouse in an unthreatening light blue. She wished she had time for a shower, but she didn't want to stretch the detective's goodwill too far. He was being pretty accommodating as it was.

When she returned to the living room, she found Michael sitting stiffly on the edge of her flower-patterned sofa with Bill and Ted wrapped around him as if he were a giant catnip toy.

"Oh, sorry," she said, walking swiftly over to rescue him from the affections of her demanding pets. She grabbed Bill off Michael's lap and set him aside, then pulled the other cat from around Michael's neck and cuddled him herself. "They're shelter cats. Deprived of affection when they were kittens, so now they demand a lot of it."

"You *are* an animal psychologist," he accused, though one corner of his mouth turned up, softening the criticism. "Do they have low self-esteem problems too?"

"No, not Bill and Ted," she said, setting Ted on the sofa and giving each cat a token scratch behind the ears. "They think a lot of themselves. You like cats?" She realized she was tense, waiting for his answer. For some stupid reason, it was important to her that he get along with her babies.

"I'm a guy. Guys aren't supposed to like cats," he hedged.

"That's a cop-out, if you'll pardon the pun."

Michael reached out reluctantly to pet Bill, who immediately abandoned Wendy's attentions for the lure of a friendly stranger. "I guess cats are okay," he admitted. "Especially big, manly boy cats like these who know how to show affection. What I can't stand are those fluffy ones with the smushed-in faces."

"You sound like you have personal experience."

He nodded. "Snow Fluff. Faye's cat. He cost four hundred dollars, ate nothing but albacore tuna, and hated me. He shredded my ostrich boots."

Wendy couldn't help it—she laughed at the mental picture he painted.

Michael scowled at her. "It's not funny. Those boots cost more than the cat did. My one indulgence."

She laughed again. "Well, Bill and Ted cost ten bucks apiece to adopt, eat bargain-basement cat food, love everyone, and they haven't developed a taste for ostrich that I know of."

"Then we'll all get along fine. You ready?"

At the reminder of the ordeal ahead of her, Wendy tensed again. "Ready as I'll ever be."

They didn't talk much on the way downtown, until Wendy asked, "Michael, do you think there's a chance, even a one-in-a-million chance, that I won't be convicted?"

"There's a huge chance you won't be convicted. You've got a great lawyer. The district attorney's office could blunder in any number of ways—"

"But if no mistakes are made?"

Michael sighed. "It looks bad for you, Wendy. What can I say?"

"And what about you?" she asked in a quiet voice. "Do you think I'm guilty?" She held her breath, waiting for his answer. It seemed to her that if, after getting to know her as he had, he still thought she was a thief, then she might as well pack it in right now, plead guilty and be done with it.

He hesitated. "Well, if I were to look strictly at the evidence—"

"No, I mean you, personally. Knowing everything you know, not just the stuff that will get into court."

"Let's just say you're not like most of the felons I've dealt with. I have a hard time believing you're a criminal. My opinion and a buck will get you a cup of coffee," he added. "Some places, anyway."

She would have to settle for that, she supposed. It was better than the cold condemnation he'd treated her to the previous day. She allowed herself to fantasize about what it would be like to have Michael Taggert on her side of the fence, supporting her a hundred percent. The idea made her warm all over.

"You're blushing again," Michael said.

"It's hot," she fibbed, reaching for the van's air conditioner controls. They were stopped at a light on the fringes of downtown, so she leaned down to study the unfamiliar switches, dials, and buttons. Could they make it any more complicated?

The moment she ducked down, a deafening crack made her ears ring. She jumped and raised up to see that her windshield had shattered. A rock must have flown up and hit it.

"I can't believe it!" she cried. "A brand-new van and the windshield can't take a little rock—"

"Get down!" Michael shouted, grabbing her by

the neck and pushing her head practically into his lap. He didn't stop there, though. With lightning-fast motions he unbuckled both of their seat belts, slid off his own seat, and dragged her to the floor of the van. Her foot couldn't help but leave the pedals.

"What are you doing?" she demanded. "We're moving!"

"It's okay, traffic will stop." He grabbed the cellular phone with one hand while pinning Wendy down with the other. She heard three blips and realized he was calling 9-1-1.

Another loud crack, and Wendy's headrest exploded into fluff. She figured out what was happening about the same time Michael verbalized it over the phone.

"This is Sergeant Michael Taggert," he said urgently into the receiver. "I'm in a green and white van at the intersection of Harry Hines and Pearl, and I'm under fire!"

She was amazingly calm, given the circumstances. Someone had shot at them with, like, real bullets. Horns were blasting at them from all sides, but no more shots were fired.

Michael released Wendy with a curt order for her to stay where she was. She turned her head just enough so that she could watch him. A gun had materialized in his hand—funny, she hadn't thought about him carrying a gun before. From his cramped, crouched position on the floor of the van, he raised up slowly, pointing his weapon in a sideways arc 180 degrees.

"Be careful," Wendy said, as if he wouldn't be at a time like this. As the van rolled to a stop, he unbent a little more, peering out first one window, then another. "Couldn't we wait for reinforcements?"

"They're here."

Wendy heard sirens—lots of them. Jeez, the whole force turned out when one of their own was threatened. The passenger door flew open and a red-faced cop peered inside.

"What the hell's going on in here?"

"We were shot at," Michael explained, flashing his badge.

"Oh, sorry, Detective Taggert, didn't realize it was you. You're causing one hell of a traffic jam. Do you think you could move the van—"

"She's not moving," he said, nodding toward Wendy, "till the area's been searched for the sniper. I'm pretty sure the shots came from that building." He pointed in a direction Wendy couldn't see.

Michael had put her safety first, which caused her already rising estimation of him to ratchet up a couple of notches. But he climbed out of his makeshift foxhole, seemingly without a care for his own well-being.

"Michael! Stay with me," she said, figuring an appeal to his protective instincts would work better than insisting he watch his own back.

But he was already out of the van. "You'll be fine," he said. "Just stay where you are." With a natural authority, he ordered one of the uniformed officers to stay with her. "Bender, get a couple of men and come with me. I'm gonna check out that building."

It seemed an eternity that Wendy waited in that uncomfortable position on the floor of her van. As the seconds and minutes ticked by, she gradually became aware of a sharp pain at her temple. She rubbed at the sore spot. Her hand came away with blood on it. She must have been cut by flying glass.

"More blood," she grumbled. "This is my day for blood." She wasn't alarmed by the minor injury itself. If it had been serious, there would have been a torrent of blood, not this little trickle. But as she probed the wound, she realized it wasn't glass that had cut her. She'd been grazed by a bullet. If she hadn't chosen that moment when the bullet flew through her windshield to study the air conditioner . . . if Michael hadn't chosen the previous moment to point out that she was blushing . . . if she hadn't chosen the moment before that to fantasize about Michael . . . The possibilities made her woozy.

"You're bleeding," her bodyguard said.

"Just a little. It's no big deal."

"Hey, we're gonna need an ambulance," the cop called. "The lady's injured."

Michael and the patrol officer named Bender had discovered nothing of interest in the building where Michael thought the shots had come from. He was forced to revise his opinion—the shots had probably been fired from a car. His mind raced, fitting puzzle pieces in place. At least two cars would have been necessary to set up the operation, one to follow and report the van's location and direction, and the other to maneuver into position to make a clean shot possible.

A sophisticated job. Unless this was a random drive-by shooting, which he doubted, not when Wendy had been nearly run down earlier. Someone was out to get her, someone who didn't want her to talk. Maybe she knew more than she thought she did.

Now that, he thought, was good, hard evidence in Wendy's favor. It was already pretty obvious, even to those who wanted to roast her, that she hadn't acted alone. But now it seemed he could make a convincing argument that she hadn't been in charge. If she was knowingly involved at all—and that was a big "if"— she was an underling, a pack mule. From there it was only a short step to the conclusion that she'd been an innocent dupe.

The first Michael knew about Wendy's injury was when he saw an ambulance pull up to the intersection where the van was still blocking traffic. The scene was bedlam, yet somehow the ambulance got through.

Michael quit ruminating about evidence and sprinted toward the van. Wendy was now sitting in the driver's seat. A cop was holding something to her head. Michael had to stop himself from dragging the cop out of the way.

"What's going on? Wendy?"

"It's nothing, Michael, just a scratch," she said, though she looked pale in the afternoon sunlight.

"Looks like she was grazed by a bullet," said the cop who was ministering to her. "There appears to be a slug in the side panel, and one definitely went through the headrest. But what I want to know is, what's all this blood in the back seat?"

"It's a long story," he replied. "But I was here, and it has nothing to do with a crime." He figured the whole story would come out later. Hell, it might even cast Wendy in a more favorable light. Today she was a true heroine, not a criminal.

Michael almost laughed, knowing what the cops must be thinking about the blood. But the sight of Wendy with that gauze pad held to her head kept him sober. He was more worried about her welfare, he realized, than he should be about a mere suspect. But then, his relationship with Wendy had advanced far beyond cop/suspect. He knew it; he just didn't want to admit it.

He liked her. He felt more alive when he was around her. In truth, he couldn't get enough of her.

"I don't want to go in the ambulance, Michael," she said. "Please. It's not necessary. The bleeding's already stopped."

"Let the paramedics take a look at her," he said to the cop, softening. If she went to the ER, it would take hours, more than she could spare. "Maybe they can treat her here."

He wanted to stay with her, but there were other pressing matters. Predictably, Lieutenant Katz from Crimes Against Persons had shown up. Though no one had been killed, shots fired in downtown Dallas in broad daylight constituted a big crime. Front-page news. And Katz loved to see his name in print.

"What the hell's going on here, Tagg?" the wiry

Katz asked in his typical no-nonsense fashion. His voice sounded as if it were being forced through a cheese grater. "Some shooter have it in for you?"

"Not me," he said quickly. "Her." He pointed to Wendy, who was now outside the van with two paramedics hovering over her.

Katz's eyes narrowed. "She that Deco Museum suspect everyone's been talking about?"

Michael nodded.

"Why would anyone be trying to kill her? Come on, Tagg, it was you they were after. You've been working on that string of burglaries in Oak Cliff. That's gang related. You've interrogated a half-dozen kids from the Pythons."

"The bullet was meant for her," Michael said again. It hadn't occurred to him that anyone would doubt Wendy was the intended victim. "She's the one who got hit."

"Since when could gang shooters aim straight?"

The lieutenant had a point there, Michael reluctantly conceded with a nod. He was willing to entertain the possibility that the bullet had been meant for him, but just barely. Wendy's earlier brush with being a hit-and-run statistic was still fresh on his mind.

"What would you say," he asked Katz, "if I told you this wasn't the first attempt on her life?" Now he had Katz's attention, so he briefly outlined the morning's events.

To his credit, Katz gave the matter some thought. Then he shook his head. "I don't buy it. You know the old saw. Look for the simplest explanation. It doesn't make sense for some hit man to go after a beautiful woman who fences jewelry."

It made sense, Michael retorted silently, if someone has a lot to protect. Michael was beginning to think Barnie Neff, or whoever he was, had more skeletons in his closet than a few burglaries. Word had gone out that Wendy was cooperating with the police. Someone, somewhere, wasn't happy with that.

Now that the adrenaline was wearing off, Wendy's head hurt. But she refused to go to the hospital. There were detectives waiting to talk to her, and she was determined to get the interrogation over with. The sooner she cooperated, the sooner the cops would find the real criminal, and she could put this whole mess behind her.

Michael had disappeared, but the nice cop who'd been assigned to watch over her offered her a ride to the station, which was only a few blocks away. She accepted, wondering what would happen to her once-shiny new van, wondering how she would get her work done without transportation.

Of course, if they didn't like her answers about the new burglaries she'd been accused of, she might not have the opportunity to work the next day. She might be in jail—again.

Could they arrest her a second time, when she'd already made bail once? It hardly seemed fair to string out these accusations, forcing her to deal with them one by one, springing a new nightmare on her just as she was coming to grips with the last one. She should call Nathaniel Mondell, she realized.

"Been a helluva day for you," the nice cop said. At least he'd let her ride in the front seat. "Didn't you just get out of jail this morning?"

This morning seemed like a lifetime ago. Since her release from jail there'd been Yoda, the near hit-and-run, the police artist, delivering a baby, an almost kiss, and getting shot. "I've had a pretty full day," she told the cop, making the biggest understatement of the year.

Her mind drifted back to the almost kiss in the hospital. Funny, but of all the events of the day, that one seemed to stick in her mind most vividly. Everything else seemed like a fuzzy, surreal movie, but she remembered the feel of Michael's hands on her, the warmth of his breath on her face, the fire in his eyes, and the answering fire in her core. . . .

She realized the cop had said something else to her. "Um, I'm sorry. What did you say?"

"I said we're here."

They were in a parking lot behind the municipal building, which housed the main police station.

"Lieutenant Katz will want to question you about the incident."

Which incident? Wendy wondered. There'd been so many.

"Aren't I supposed to talk to some burglary detective?" she asked. "They think I ripped off some of my clients."

"Wow. Sounds like you've been busy."

"I didn't *do* any of the stuff they think I did," she snapped. "It's just a big misunderstanding."

"Yeah, that's what they all say," the cop said affably. Suddenly she didn't think he was so nice anymore, and she realized he hadn't been assigned to her as a courtesy, but as a security measure. They still thought she was going to flee.

She ended up talking to both a CAPers—Crimes Against Persons—detective and a couple of men from Theft, compatriots of Michael's, no doubt. It took the rest of the day. She'd hoped Michael would turn up again, but she didn't catch even a glimpse of him during all the arduous hours she spent answering questions.

She did manage to get hold of Nathaniel Mondell, who made everything take twice as long because he wouldn't let her give a straight answer to anything. Sometimes she thought she would be better off without him and his confrontational attitude. He tended to get the cops' ire up by his very presence. But she knew so little about her legal rights that she decided to bow to his judgment. The mayor had recommended Mondell highly, so he must be good.

The burglary guys were about done chewing her up and spitting her out. She hadn't fared too well during the interrogation. She'd checked her organizer for all of the dates on which the burglaries had occurred. All had been on weeknights, and, as it turned out, she hadn't spent any of those nights with James. She didn't have an alibi for a single one.

"Home alone, all by yourself. No phone calls?

Pizza delivery, maybe?" one of the detectives had said with a sneer.

"I'm usually asleep, alone, at two in the morning," she'd ground out, seeing no need to bring up James now that he couldn't do her any good. "I don't talk on the phone or eat pizza in the middle of the night!"

Mondell had shaken his head slightly, indicating she needed to get control of her emotions. Losing it wouldn't help her case, and that's exactly what the detectives were after.

She'd forced herself to be calm, only to get worked up again when they'd tried to pressure her into giving up the names of her associates, or partners in crime, or bosses, or whatever. Shades of the Salem witch trials, she thought, and asked when they would break out the thumb screws.

"I wonder how many suspects blurt out any old name just to get you guys to ease up?" she asked. "For the last time, I don't know any thieves or criminals or fences or burglars. The only person I know is Barnie Neff, and I've told you everything I can think of about him."

That was when Michael finally showed up with a sheaf of papers in hand, and she'd never been so glad to see anyone in her life, though she wasn't sure why. She supposed it was because he was the only person around who didn't look at her as if she were a piece of gum on the underside of a theater seat.

She leaped out of her chair with the full intention of throwing her arms around him. Only when he gave a barely imperceptible shake of his head did she realize what she'd been about to do. Embracing the detective who'd first arrested her would have looked very strange.

One detective who'd been interrogating her— Smythe, she thought his name was—gave Michael a nod. "You have anything to add to this, Tagg?"

"Yeah. I think the lady's been set up." He handed a piece of paper to each of the other detectives. "This guy look familiar to either of you?"

Smythe snorted. "This is the artist's composite?"

"Yeah," Michael said.

The other detective, whose name escaped Wendy, set the drawing aside with hardly a second glance. "Could be anyone. Hell, he even looks a little bit like Captain Patterson, except for the chin."

Smythe brayed like a donkey at that suggestion, and even Michael fought a smile.

"I'm glad you all think this is so funny," Wendy said. "But that drawing isn't of just anyone. It looks like Barnie Neff. Don't you guys have some books of mug shots or something I could look through?"

The levity receded.

"That's an excellent suggestion, Ms. Thayer," Michael said. She hated it that he'd reverted to such a formal title for her. It made her feel like the closeness they'd shared that day was somehow wrong, that they had to deny it, hide it from the world. Granted, they couldn't become involved, but was there some law that said she couldn't become friends with a cop who was investigating her?

She supposed there was. He'd already gone out of

his way to help her. Not that he would ever suppress evidence or do anything unethical to get her off the hook, but if he cozied up to a suspect, it wouldn't reflect well on him.

Mondell spoke up again. "I've been suggesting that Ms. Thayer look at mug shots since yesterday," he said huffily. Wendy didn't remember any mention of mug shots until now, from him or anyone, but she'd give him credit for turning every possible circumstance their way. "Could it be that once you have a suspect, you'd rather not have any more leads to follow? Makes it hard to railroad an innocent person into jail if there are unanswered questions, other suspects, right?"

"This investigation is proceeding like any other," Smythe said, rising to Mondell's bait. "First the questions, then the mug shots. I can't speak for what happened last night, since I wasn't here."

Just then Wendy got a whiff of popcorn from someplace, and her stomach growled. She realized she hadn't eaten since that lousy dinner they'd fed her in jail the night before. As fast as she burned up energy, she didn't do well without a regular intake of calories.

"You guys done with her?" Michael asked the other two detectives. "If so, I'll show her the mug shots."

"Yeah, go ahead," Smythe said.

"You gonna charge her?" Michael asked casually.

Wendy tensed. Smythe gave her a sharp look. "Not yet. But we have loads of physical evidence from those burglaries. Soon as we find a match with the shopping queen here, she's toast. Unless she works with us."

On that note he left, taking his partner with him.

"You can go, too, Nathaniel," Wendy said to her lawyer. "I'm sure you have dinner plans."

"I think I should stay with you," he said, though without much conviction.

"I'll be fine. Don't run the bill up any higher than it already is, okay?" She smiled, letting him know she was teasing. "I spent almost the entire day with Detective Taggert here. If I were going to incriminate myself in front of him, I'd have done it already."

Nathaniel smiled back. He really did have a pleasant face when he smiled. "All right. If you're sure."

After he left, and she was alone with Michael, she couldn't contain herself anymore. "I have to eat something," she said. "A candy bar, potato chips, anything. You must be hungry too. We skipped lunch."

Michael looked down at his shoes guiltily. "I grabbed a handful of doughnuts in the break room. Tell you what. I'll get us some burgers—"

"Oh, wait." She opened her purse, retrieved her coupon organizer, and quickly riffled through it. "There's a Big Sid's Deli across the street, right? I have a dollar-off coupon. Turkey and Swiss on rye for me, and you can get anything you want, except don't get the pastrami. It's fatty and too expensive. I can start on the mug shots."

Michael smiled. "You're bossy, you know that?"

"I prefer to think of it as a take-charge attitude," she said, only slightly offended. "I loathe dithering, so

I make decisions. You're free to challenge. I keep an open mind."

"Big Sid's is fine." He led her through a rabbit warren of offices, cubicles, bunched desks, and partitions. There didn't seem to be any rhyme or reason to how the work stations were arranged. There was no discernible decor. Battleship gray, imitation wood tone, and mauve burlap partitions were all grouped together in a riotous conglomeration.

She'd go crazy working there. Not only was it disorganized, but every desk seemed to have piles of paper on it. It was a wonder the police department functioned at all.

Finally they arrived at a back room with row upon row of filing cabinets. Against one wall were shelves filled with binders, labeled with various crimes: burglary, car theft, rape, murder, fraud. Michael grabbed a stack of the burglary binders, cleared off a space on a little table, and set them down. "Start at the back— they're more recent. I'll be back in a few with the grub."

She was actually glad for those few minutes of solitude he gave her—well, solitude if you didn't count the thousands of felons in the binders, a new gallery of beady eyes staring at her with each page she turned. She wished she could just close her eyes and meditate for a few minutes, but she didn't have the time. She had to find Barnie Neff.

She would know him if she saw him—in an instant. But it would take her a week to look at all the mug shots. Well, the sooner she started, the sooner she'd be done.

The smell of chili fries reached her before Michael did. Her stomach rumbled again. She was light-headed, and all those little postage-stamp-size pictures were starting to run together.

"Any luck?" Michael asked, setting down a white bag and a large cola in front of her. Another bag held the steaming chili fries.

"I haven't even come close," she said. "But I've got lots more pictures to go through."

"Take your time."

She unwrapped her sandwich and bit into it. No food had ever tasted so good. The cola was cold and sweet.

"You know, I don't want to alarm you," Michael said, "but we need to think about your safety. Some-one's trying to kill you."

She looked up at him, surprised that he'd stated the possibility so baldly. "Oh, I don't think so."

"I do. That car almost ran you over earlier—"

"That was my fault. I didn't look where I was go-ing."

"Yeah, well, the bullet through your windshield wasn't your fault."

"I was assuming that was some sort of random thing. Like that guy several years ago who stood on a highway overpass and started randomly shooting at cars."

Michael shook his head. "You're in denial. One

brush with death I might dismiss as chance, but not two in one day. Someone's got your number, sweets."

She took an inappropriate amount of pleasure in the casual endearment. Michael Taggert had quickly become an important fixture in her life.

"You really think so?" she said, pondering the possibility that someone wanted her dead. "I mean, that guy who questioned me earlier didn't take that angle. He didn't ask if anyone was mad at me or if I had any enemies."

"Lieutenant Katz, you mean."

She shrugged. "All the names are running together at this point."

"Katz thinks the shooter was after me."

"Maybe he was."

"He hit you, though. Whatever, I don't think you should take any chances."

"What am I supposed to do? Hire a bodyguard?"

Apparently Michael had already thought of that. "I tried to get someone assigned to protect you, but my captain wouldn't go for it. Not in the budget, no urgent need, yada yada yada."

"So what's the alternative?"

"Hide. Stay someplace where Neff, or whoever it is, can't find you."

"Maybe I should just take my bail back and let them put me in jail," she said, only half joking.

Michael shook his head. "Jail's not that safe."

"I can't afford a hotel, and I'm not putting any of my friends or family in danger by shacking up with them."

Michael thought for a moment. "You have a gun?"

"Heavens, no! I hate guns."

"Does your apartment have a security alarm?"

"No."

He thought again. When he spoke, his voice was lowered to a conspiratorial whisper. "Okay, here's the deal. I'll give you a safe place to stay, but you can't tell anyone. The D.A.'s office would frown on it."

SIX

Maybe it was because it had been the longest day in history, but Wendy's first impulse was to jump at Michael's offer. A safe place, just for one night. She hadn't felt safe since her arrest.

But exactly how safe would she be with the dangerously handsome detective who made her think, and sometimes do, such crazy things? So she forced herself to move cautiously.

"You want me to . . . go home with you?"

His reaction was immediate and emphatic. "Oh, no, hell, no," he said, actually backing away from her. "That wouldn't be kosher at all. No, see, I've got a furnished rental house—empty right now—in Oak Cliff. It's not much, but it's clean and has good locks and a security alarm."

It sounded like heaven, almost too good to be true. If only the furnishings included one Michael Taggert to watch over her. Okay, she was acting like a goofball, but she felt pretty fragile right now. Nearly getting killed twice in one day could do that, she reasoned, cutting herself some slack.

"How will we get there?" she asked, amazed that she could still think along practical lines.

"I have a car—my car, not a police vehicle. I'll take you out through the garage. No one will know where to find you except me."

The mention of cars made her remember her poor van, which had been so sparkling new a few days earlier. It had been impounded as evidence, and she didn't think the police department would be kind enough to provide her with a loaner. How was she going to get her work done in the days to come?

Like Scarlett O'Hara, she would deal with that tomorrow.

She squared her shoulders and tried to pretend that Michael's offer was just another thoughtful gesture, not a wild aberration of police policy. She also tried not to think about what it really meant, if anything.

"Okay," she said. "It's decent of you to offer. Just let me look through a few more of these photos." She propped her chin in her hands and resumed her study of the mug shot book. Her eyes were bleary, though. The faces were running together. She wasn't so sure anymore that she could immediately spot Mr. Neff.

Michael came up behind her and put his hands on her shoulders. "Wendy. You can try again tomorrow. Let it go for now so you can get some sleep."

Boy, that sounded good. He didn't need to ask her

twice. She gathered up the refuse from their dinner and pitched it, then followed Michael toward the Municipal Building's garage, feeling frustrated and exhausted.

But behind those negative feelings, like a seed in the hard winter ground, she felt a morsel of happiness too. It had something to do with Michael, she knew. If he hadn't taken an interest in her, if she didn't have him to talk to and bounce ideas off of, she would be completely lost.

Yet she knew she had to be careful. Maybe he was cozying up to her for a reason. Maybe it was all an act, engineered so that Michael would gain her trust and she would confide in him, or slip up. She knew that cops played all kinds of nasty tricks on suspects—sting operations, entrapment schemes, promises never meant to be kept.

She knew what Nathaniel would say if he found out she was letting the investigating detective put her up for the night. He wouldn't be pleased, to say the least. Or maybe he'd somehow turn Michael's offer into something that would work *for* her. She could see him playing it up before a jury, making it sound like Michael intended to compromise her or harass her or something.

Well, it didn't matter. What Nathaniel didn't know wouldn't hurt him. Hopefully it wouldn't hurt her, either.

Michael led her through the parking garage to his vehicle, a white Firebird that had to be at least twenty years old. It was a classic—or it would have been if it didn't have two crumpled fenders and one red door.

"Now, this is an inconspicuous car," she quipped when he opened the passenger door for her.

"Hey, it gets me where I need to go."

As she sank into the bucket seat, she wondered what they were paying detectives these days.

He was attuned to her train of thought. "Every spare penny during the last seven years has gone to pay off Faye's debts," he explained. "Didn't leave a lot of room for luxury cars." He started the engine. Unlike his police sedan, the Firebird had an engine that purred.

"Why didn't you declare bankruptcy?" she asked.

He shrugged. "I thought about it, but it didn't sit well with me. I believe in taking responsibility for my mistakes."

"Yes, but that debt was your ex-wife's mistake, not yours," Wendy pointed out.

"My mistake was marrying her," he said, sounding a little melancholy. "Anyway, it's a done deal now. As of last month I'm free and clear of debt. I'm gonna get this baby some body work and a paint job. Might even paint her red. Candy apple red."

Wendy smiled. Hearing him share a fantasy, even a minor one, filled her with warmth. "I know a body shop that does great work. In fact, the guy who owns it is an ex-cop. I bet he'd give you a law enforcement discount. He did the logo on my van and let me trade it out in errands."

"I kinda figured you'd know someone," he said with a lazy smile.

Oak Cliff wasn't a suburb, exactly. It was a small town that had grown up side by side with Dallas, eventually to be swallowed up and incorporated by the larger city. It was a conglomoration of neighborhoods with strong individual identities—Winnetka Heights, Kidd Springs, Kessler Park. Many of the Dallas area's oldest homes stood there—some gloriously renovated, many looking as though they were about to fall down.

Michael's rental house, in the well-to-do Kessler Park neighborhood, was really quite nice, Wendy decided as they pulled into the driveway. A fifties bungalow of native limestone, it sported freshly painted trim and a neatly landscaped yard. The front porch looked as if it had just been swept.

"You're sure it's empty?" she asked. "Looks lived in to me."

"The neighbor looks after the place when I don't have renters," he explained. "My last tenants moved out without warning a couple of weeks ago, and I haven't had a chance to advertise for new ones."

She followed him up to the porch and waited while he wrestled with a contrary lock. "How'd you end up with this cute little house?" she asked.

"Actually it belongs to my grandparents," he answered. "They're in a nursing home. The rental income helps with the bills, a little."

"You take care of them?" she asked, adjusting her thinking again. She hadn't thought of Michael Taggert as having a family, friends, or any life outside his police work. She hadn't, as a matter of fact, even considered that he might have a current wife in addition to the shopaholic ex. He didn't wear a ring, but lots of men didn't.

"My brother and I help out when we can."

"Where are your parents?" she thought to ask.

"Dead," he replied. "They both died young, in their fifties. Natural causes."

He finally got the key to turn and opened the front door. A musty, unused smell greeted them as they entered.

Whatever could be called charming about the house ended at the threshold. Brown sculptured carpeting spread out like mold across all available floors, and Wendy suspected the stale odor emanated from them. The furniture was horrific, bland and boxy and also brown. The walls were dingy white, sorely in need of paint. Plastic pull-down shades were the only window treatments.

"I warned you," he said.

She couldn't think of anything to say that was complimentary, so she remained silent.

"Bedrooms are back here," he said, leading her down a dark hallway, flipping on lights as he went.

The master bedroom was small and dark even with the lights on. The double bed had a bare mattress that sagged visibly in the middle, but at least it looked clean.

"Mattress Giant has a sale on next weekend," she said helpfully.

Either he didn't hear or chose to ignore her suggestion. He was rummaging around in a hall cupboard. "Sheets," he explained, producing a set of plain white linens.

"How do you ever find renters?" she blurted out.

He chose to interpret her question as honest curiosity. "Same way anyone else does it. Ads in the newspaper, word of mouth. Why, do you know someone who needs a two-bedroom house? The rent's cheap for this area, and it's an easy drive downtown."

"You could get higher rent if you redecorated," she pointed out.

He looked around, a thoughtful scowl on his face. "Is it really that bad?"

"It's worse than bad. Not that I'm ungrateful, mind you. I'm ecstatic to have a place to stay where I don't have to worry about gunfire coming through the windows." She shivered at the thought. "I was just thinking. Since you're doing me a favor, I could return it by redecorating. Nothing major, just a little paint and paper, slipcovers, maybe some throw rugs, miniblinds."

She couldn't help herself. To her, this place was like a hideous painting was to an artist. The artist could whitewash over the canvas and start again. That's what she'd like to do.

He shook his head. "I don't think I can afford your fees."

"I said a *favor*. I won't charge you," she said, irritated that he thought she wanted to make a quick buck off him. "You just pay me for the raw materials, which, of course, I will get you fabulous bargains on."

Michael nodded absently. "Yeah, sure, we can talk about it. But you don't need to repay me. I'm doing myself a favor as well as you. I have to keep you safe or the mayor will have me roasted alive. So much for the FBI."

"Why do you want to work for the FBI?" she asked, now insatiably curious. He didn't usually talk about himself, and she wanted to take avantage of the fact that he'd let his guard down.

He shrugged. "A change. Higher pay, more excitement."

"More excitement than getting shot at?"

"This has been an unusual day," he said, tossing her a couple of pillowcases. "I've never been shot at before."

"So you'd be some kind of special agent, chasing down America's Most Wanted and all that?"

"Actually, I was kidding about the excitement. I was recruited for a desk job, doing statistical analysis."

"Crunching numbers."

"Yeah. Analyzing crime patterns, helping to allocate resources."

"Michael, no offense, but that sounds really boring."

"It's what I studied in college. I'm good at it."

"But is that what you'd really enjoy? Locking yourself in some basement cubbyhole with a computer and spreadsheets?"

"It's not like that, I'm sure."

"But—"

"Listen. I'm thirty-five and going nowhere in the

DPD. I keep putting my application in to work in CAPers, and they keep kicking it back, citing a long list of excuses. But it comes down to politics. I don't play the political games or curry favor with the right people."

"You sure ticked off the mayor," she said.

"I gotta get out of Dallas, move up, make a name for myself."

"You think it'll be any different working for the federal government? I bet at the FBI you'll have to kiss someone's butt just to get a password to your computer."

He shrugged, clearly uncomfortable with her logic.

In truth, she didn't know anything about working for the FBI. But she didn't like the thought of him leaving town forever. "Where will you be stationed?"

"Washington."

"Who will take care of your grandparents' house?" she asked.

"My brother. I've worked it out." Now he was getting cross with her. She'd touched a nerve. Foisting the rental house off on his brother didn't jibe with the man she was coming to know.

They finished making the bed in silence. She tried to think of something that would prolong his staying with her. She was a little afraid to be alone. The only thing that came to mind was to work out logistics.

"Can you drop me off at my office tomorrow, or should I call a cab?" she asked brightly. She didn't want to put him out any more than she already had.

He sank onto the edge of her bed. Wendy's heart

beat faster, seeing him there in that place where she would be spending the night. "Wendy, I don't think you should work tomorrow."

"Oh, but I have to," she said. "I have a completely full schedule, plus whatever requests Jillian took in today. My gosh, she probably wonders what happened to me. I'll have to call her at home. Is there a phone?"

He pulled a tiny cellular from his shirt pocket and laid it on the nightstand.

"Thanks." She started to reach for it.

He laid a hand on her arm, stilling her. "Slow down a minute, Wendy. Think. Need I remind you that there's someone out there who wants you dead?"

She folded her arms. "I can't let my business fall apart. I've worked too hard to get where I am."

"You can't put your life at risk," he said flatly.

That got her back up. What he said made perfect sense, but it was the way he said it that annoyed her. Did he think he had the right to boss her around just because he'd been nice to her?

"I will do whatever I need to do in order not to hurt my reputation or disappoint my clients," she said smoothly. "You can't hold me prisoner here. I made bail, remember?"

Michael stared at her. He didn't have to say a thing. Her smart-aleck arguments evaporated like dew on a sunny morning.

"Okay, fine. I can always start another business." She shrugged. "I'll call Jillian."

He sat close to the phone, so she almost had to

reach around him to pick it up. She felt the heat from his body.

"Wait," he said, touching her arm yet again. "I have tomorrow off. I can do your shopping and errands for you."

Wendy broke into peals of laughter. "You? A personal shopper?"

"I watched you do it yesterday. It didn't look all that hard. Tell this Jillian I'm a new employee. She can give me the easy stuff, like dog walking and picking up dry cleaning."

Oh, Lord, he was serious. Maybe she should be serious, too, she reasoned. He was only trying to help her keep her business afloat. She couldn't see him selecting women's apparel or putting together a gourmet meal any more than she could see herself arresting and interrogating suspects. But he could drop off and pick up stuff as well as anyone, and she figured she could count on him to be honest.

"All right," she said. "I'll even pay you, how's that?"

He shrugged. "It's not necessary, but if it'll make you feel better, okay."

It did. His list of favors for her was growing. She didn't want to be any more beholden to him than she already was.

"But," she added, "I dare you to claim my job's 'not that hard' after you spend a day doing it."

He grinned. "Piece of cake." Then he gave her a look of mock cowardice. "You won't make me walk Yoda, will you?" He cringed dramatically.

"I only do Yoda once a week," she said. "But I think I'll give you the Poms." She didn't explain, wanting him to worry a bit.

Michael couldn't think of any reason to stay longer. Wendy was settled in; she had his instructions for what to do if there was trouble; she knew how to use the security system; she had his cell phone and the charger. He offered to let her keep his extra gun, but she would have none of that.

"That would be stooping to Mr. Neff's level," she said. "Besides, I'm scared of guns."

Michael didn't press it. If she was hesitant to fire a gun—and most people were—there was too great a chance a bad guy could use the weapon against her.

"Don't hesitate to call 9-1-1," he said, continuing with his litany of warnings, "though I'm positive no one followed us here."

"I won't."

"I'll check in with you tomorrow, then." He started out the bedroom door.

"Oh, Michael?"

"Yeah?"

"What about the investigation? What's being done?"

He sighed. This was where his ethical footing got a little dicey. "Technically, I'm supposed to be gathering evidence to turn over to the D.A.'s office."

"So they can put me away."

"Yeah. But I'm also supposed to follow all leads,

not just the ones that make you look guilty. So I did some follow-up with the artist's composite, showing it around, trying to get the papers to run it."

"And will they?"

He shook his head. "Neither will the TV stations. The media got stung a few months ago when they plastered the city with the composite of a 'suspect' that turned out to be the figment of a guilty witness's imagination."

She nodded. "I remember that. The police department was a little embarrassed, too, if I recall."

"Yeah. So no one's that anxious to push Linda's rendering of Mr. Neff—especially since it looks a little like Captain Patterson, the guy the mayor's giving the retirement party for."

Wendy gasped. "Oooh, that's right, the mayor's party. I have some major stuff to take care of." She sagged. "I guess I can do some of it on the phone. Um, what else?"

"I've got the name of the person at the bank who opened Mr. Neff's account. I'll see if her description matches yours."

"If she even remembers," Wendy said glumly. "I'll bet he's had that account for months. She's probably opened a hundred accounts since then. What else?"

"Motor Vehicles is tracking down the brown car. I got a partial license number on it."

"You're actually doing quite a bit," she said, sounding surprised.

"I've also been digging into your background," he admitted. "Prior arrests, stuff like that."

"I've never been arrest—oh, wait a minute."

"I know all about it, Wendy," he said with mock seriousness. "Chaining yourself to a tree. Really. How sixties."

"It was one of the oldest trees in my neighborhood!"

"I read the article. Don't worry, the D.A. can't make much of that. Are there any other skeletons in your closet I should worry about?"

"The rest of my skeletons are buried too deep to find," she said mysteriously. He couldn't tell whether she was joking or not.

The old man couldn't sleep. He sat up, pushed himself out of bed, and lit a cigarette. At the rate he'd been smoking lately, he really *would* have emphysema. But he tended to smoke a lot when he was worried.

Wendy Thayer was proving the proverbial thorn in his side. First, she hadn't deposited the money from fencing the deco jewelry. That was a loss of several thousand dollars.

Second, she'd eluded a professional hit not once, but twice. The hit-and-run attempt was sloppy, he had to admit. But how she'd managed to live through the second attempt on her life was astounding. She'd been struck, his sources told him, but apparently her injuries had been so slight that she hadn't even gone to the hospital.

Third, she was missing, location unknown. She'd

gone to ground, and now that she was on the alert, getting rid of her would be twice as hard.

Funny, but she didn't remind him in the least of his sister anymore. And he wouldn't regret dispatching her. She was dangerous to him.

He had only three days to go, three wretched days before he was on a midnight plane headed for Tahiti, and paradise was his. Savagely he stubbed out his cigarette. He wasn't about to let some little shopper girl ruin it for him.

SEVEN

"Hi, I'm the new guy," Michael said pleasantly to the petite woman behind the desk at Born to Shop. This, presumably, was Jillian. "Here's the master key ring," he added. "Wendy said you were to be the mistress of the keys for the day."

Jillian smiled and took the key ring. "Hi. I didn't even know Wendy was looking for someone new until she called me last night. And, wow, a guy, too. You're the first guy she's ever hired."

"She doesn't want to be sued for sex discrimination," he said, tongue firmly in cheek. "Guys can shop."

"Oh, I'm sure *you* can, or she wouldn't have hired you." She handed him a thick sheaf of papers. "I typed it all out for you." As she talked, she consulted a list on her computer and removed certain keys from the ring. These she handed to Michael, along with an envelope containing various claim tickets.

"There's only one place with a security alarm. It's written down for you."

"Thanks." He eyed the computer thoughtfully. "You have access to a lot of information in that computer, I bet," he said, trying his best to sound conversational.

Jillian nodded. "Wendy gave me the password last night." She smiled mischievously. "She doesn't realize I already figured it out." She lowered her voice. "It's her birth date."

Inwardly, Michael groaned. Didn't Wendy know better than to use something so easy to figure out for a password? If Jillian knew the password, probably everyone who worked there did. Mr. Neff could have gotten it from an employee. More than likely, though, he'd figured it out for himself. He could have gotten into Wendy's apartment any day of the week and had hours to make guesses.

"Call in every couple of hours, okay?" Jillian said. "I might have something else for you later. You have a city map book, right?" she asked. Every cop had one. His was in his ailing police car.

"Um, no."

She handed him a much-frayed green and yellow book. "This one's mine. Lose it and you're dead meat. You'll have to buy one of your own, but Wendy will reimburse you for it."

He nodded, then glanced down at the papers. If he had questions, he figured it would be better to ask them now. As he scanned the list of errands, he felt his eyes glazing over.

"What is this, a week's worth?"

Jillian obviously thought he was kidding. "You'll do fine. The first day is always the worst. I used to run errands before I got promoted to office manager."

"Hey, that's a great idea. I'll stay and answer the phone, and you can run—"

Jillian held up her hand. "Not a chance. No one talks me out of my cushy office job. Now get out of here." She wadded up a piece of scratch paper and threw it at him. "Don't come back till you've shopped till you drop. That's our motto."

Michael saluted her and turned for the door, not feeling nearly as confident as he had the night before. Piece of cake indeed. He didn't even have an organizer.

Wendy sat at the chipped Formica table eating some toaster waffles. Everywhere she looked, she was reminded of how dreadfully this house needed a new decor.

She'd walked down to the corner for a newspaper. She hadn't read one in a couple of days, which made her antsy.

The first thing she did was check to see if there was any mention of her arrest. She made it through the front section and breathed a sigh of relief. Then she dropped her fork.

There it was, right on the front page of the Metropolitan section, and they even had a picture.

How horrible. How humiliating. No, not just humiliating, *devastating*. Her clients would drop away like rats deserting a sinking ship, and could she blame them? She wouldn't want to leave her valuables or belongings with a suspected felon.

She took a deep breath and tried to put this fiasco into perspective. She'd known this would happen sooner or later. In fact, she was frankly surprised some reporter hadn't found her name on the police blotter and run the story yesterday.

The adverse publicity could cripple her business, she thought grimly. Even after she cleared herself, she might never recover. Then again, she'd always heard that any publicity was good, anything that got your name in front of the public. Her newfound notoriety could be a double-edged sword. And if she managed to clear herself and find the real museum thief, public opinion toward her might turn favorable.

She could hope. She was nothing if not optimistic.

She scanned the article. Michael was quoted, of course. What he said about her was mostly benign— that she was a suspect, that the investigation was continuing, that nothing had been proven yet. Detective Smythe, the one investigating the home break-ins, was less circumspect.

The reporter did at least mention the mysterious Barnie Neff and cited the evidence that such a person existed, but they didn't physically describe him or ask readers for help in identifying him.

Wendy turned her attention to her picture, a file photo taken several years ago when she'd helped organize a charity auction, an activity one of her wealthy friends had lured her into. The likeness was less than flattering. She looked harsh, and she wasn't smiling. Gee, if the paper had wanted a photo, she'd have gladly provided them with one of her glamorous publicity photos.

Enough of the pity party, she decided. First she would call Jillian and warn her to expect a barrage of cancellations. Then she would call the newspaper reporter and offer her side of the story. No, wait, Nathaniel had warned her not to talk to the media.

She flipped to the inside of the Met section, and her breath caught in her throat. Fabric-a-rama was having its semiannual clearance sale! And there was a location on Jefferson Street only about six blocks from Michael's rental house.

She had to do something. She couldn't just sit and twiddle her thumbs. There wasn't even a television, not that she'd watch it if there was one. And Michael had said she could redecorate. Oh, not precisely. He'd said they could talk about it. But she was sure he would like what she did, and she would assume the risk.

She started making a list.

Michael was less than a third of the way through his list of errands, and it was almost one o'clock. He could see he wouldn't be taking a lunch break.

What had possessed him to think this job was easy? The Poms—a pair of yippy Pomeranian dogs from hell—had scratched his leather upholstery on the way to the groomers. He'd picked up a cake for a party from a bakery, then had upended it in the parking lot and was forced to pay for a replacement from his own pocket. He'd have to pick it up later that afternoon.

Taking some guy's Lexus in for an oil change hadn't sounded too hard, until he'd found a waiting line ten cars long. No way could he wait. He'd left the car there and jogged the mile and a half back to the guy's office, where his own car was parked, explaining to the client that he would have to pick up the car later. The client hadn't been too pleased.

He'd done the grocery shopping for a nice little old lady who'd provided him with a detailed list, but he was unfamiliar with her neighborhood store and it took him an hour to find everything. Then she complained that he'd gotten the wrong brand of bran flakes and laundry detergent. He soothed her by taking those items off her bill. He'd pay for them out of his own pocket.

He'd had to pick up two watches at two different jewelry stores and deliver them to their owners' homes. He'd realized, as he was delivering the second one, that he'd gotten the watches mixed up. He had to backtrack.

Wendy enjoyed this? he thought. This was his idea of hell.

By two o'clock he'd made up some of the lost time by driving like a maniac. He was starving, so he stopped for a bagel.

That was when he read the newspaper.

Poor Wendy. He'd tried to downplay the story for

the reporter, as if it wasn't any big deal, but he supposed his snow job hadn't worked.

He pictured Wendy at home in his rental house, blissfully ignorant of the day's news. He hoped she would take this opportunity to rest, sleep in, read a book. She would probably talk to Jillian eventually and find out about the article, but he hoped it was later rather than sooner.

He didn't know when Wendy Thayer had gotten under his skin, but she was definitely there now. He wasn't sure when he'd started to believe she was innocent, but the fact of the matter was, he couldn't see her jaywalking, much less breaking into a museum or fencing stolen merchandise. She was too . . . too what? Nice? Sweet? Guileless? Innocent?

No, those words didn't begin to describe Wendy. She was too . . . sexy. That was it. Too sexy to be a felon.

He shook his head, calling himself ten kinds of idiot. Was he was falling for the oldest trick in the book, letting a beautiful woman bamboozle him into thinking she was innocent just because she fluttered her eyelashes at him and seemed oh-so-overwhelmed by the mean old criminal justice system?

Maybe he was that stupid. But he hadn't imagined that brown Caprice, or the speeding bullet that could have ended her life. That reminded him—he needed to call Joe.

On his way to a nearby department store to pick up concert tickets, he punched in the number on a spare cellular Jillian had given him.

"Joe Gaglione," his partner intoned in a bored voice.

"Joe. You got any information on that brown Caprice?"

Joe chuckled. "It's a more common car than you thought, Tagg. I have eight of them."

"You're kidding. But with the license number—"

"Partial license number. You only got the first three letters, you know."

"Yeah, but you should still be able to narrow it down."

Joe chuckled again. "Ordinarily. But you know how every couple of years the police department auctions off its outdated cruisers?"

"Yeah . . ."

"It so happens that in 1992 we auctioned off twelve of the suckers. All Caprices. Every one of 'em was painted a nice, neutral brown before the auction."

Michael groaned. He knew what was coming next.

"They licensed them all at the same time, so the numbers—"

"—are in sequence," Michael finished for him.

Joe continued his report, obviously enjoying his partner's consternation. "Of those twelve that were auctioned, eight are still on the road in Dallas."

"Do you have time to track any down?"

Joe sighed. "I got some hot cases, man. Anyway, what are you doing? I thought you were putting in some overtime today."

That had been the plan, until he'd realized how badly Wendy needed a hand. "Something came up.

Fax the list to my house, okay? I'll start making calls tonight."

Wendy stepped back to admire her handiwork. Had she gone too far? She didn't think so, but she chewed on her lip, hoping Michael would agree.

She'd found some gorgeous fabric remnants on sale for seventy-five cents a yard—unheard of, even at Fabric-a-rama's semiannual sale. She could put together no-sew window treatments with rubber bands and safety pins in the blink of an eye. The plastic shades came down, replaced by white sheers. Okay, so each window had a different fabric. She'd coordinated as best she could, and the effect looked deliberately eclectic.

But she hadn't stopped there. A cute little hardware store on Jefferson had some paint on sale. The walls in the living room were now a pale celery green.

Out of curiosity she'd pulled up a corner of the ghastly carpet to discover pristine hardwoods underneath. They didn't even need sanding. The carpet was so old that a good yank was all it took to get rid of it. It was now heaped in the garage.

A couple of throw rugs from the Salvation Army Thrift Store—seven bucks each—kept the floors from looking too stark. Also from the thrift store, some Victorian-style prints of birds and flowers she'd found stuck in a bookcase. Framing them would have been more than she wanted to spend without Michael's okay, so she'd thumbtacked them onto the bare walls.

The furniture needed reupholstering. Better still, it needed to be heaved onto the nearest trash heap. So she'd camouflaged the ugly brown color and boxy lines with some soft, pastel throws and pillows.

She'd finished the redecorating with herself. She'd sorely needed a change of clothes, so she'd bought a work shirt and a pair of jeans from a Western store.

She smiled delightedly. Michael would be shocked, but he couldn't fail to be pleased with how little money she'd spent on his renovations.

Now that she was done with her frenetic activity, though, she couldn't avoid her real problems any longer. She'd talked to Jillian, several times. A number of her clients, mostly newer ones who hadn't known her long, called Born to Shop to announce that they wouldn't be needing the company's services any longer.

On the other hand, they'd had a little flurry of new customers. Of course, Jillian hadn't mentioned the newspaper article to anyone who hadn't brought it up first, but Wendy had to wonder if the new business was a result of the bad publicity. Some people were fascinated with notoriety of any kind and would do anything to get close to it.

A sound at the front door made her jump. Though she'd managed to forget it for a while, the reality hit her anew: Someone wanted to kill her.

"Who's there?" she called out, already reaching for the cell phone, which she'd kept in her pocket all day.

"It's me, Michael," her visitor called through the door. "The damn key is sticking."

Relief poured through her. She opened the dead bolt and flung the door open, feeling suddenly nervous over Michael's return—like a new wife who'd done something to the house and hoped for her husband's approval.

She pushed the silly thought aside and stood behind the door to allow Michael inside.

"Wendy? I—uh, oh, sorry, wrong house. No wonder the key didn't work." He backed across the threshold and onto the porch. She watched him through the narrow window to the side of the door, smiling as he checked the house number, then looked up and down the street. His handsome face was a mask of confusion.

He opened the door again. "Wendy?"

"Right here."

He came inside and closed the door, trying to look everywhere at once. "Did I just enter the Twilight Zone?"

She laughed. "I was bored, so I did a little redecorating. Now, you might not agree with my taste—"

He turned on her like a ticked-off Doberman pinscher. "Wendy, what were you thinking?" He grabbed her by the shoulders, and she could tell he was trying to resist a mighty urge to shake her.

Her heart hammered inside her chest. "You don't like it, you don't have to pay for it," she said in a small voice. "I'll take it all down."

"It's not that I—how did you do all this in one day?" He wasn't backing down at all.

"I just walked down to that strip shopping center—"

"I *knew* it! You left the house. You made yourself a perfect target. Wendy, Wendy, how could you be that careless with your life?" He crushed her against him, and all at once Wendy realized this had nothing to do with her taste in decor. Michael was angry because she'd put herself in danger.

"But no one knew where I was," she defended herself, though she wasn't sure he could understand her. Her face was mashed against his chest.

"Someone could have found out. I told you not to leave the house."

"You didn't," she countered.

"Then I should have. I guess I assumed you had an ounce of common sense."

She reared back, struggling against his embrace. "Now, you listen here—"

"No, you listen. I'm trying to keep you safe. I've put my career, my whole future, on the line by helping you, and you—"

"You put my career on the line when you arrested me! Now you're just trying to cover your butt!" Even as she said it, she knew it wasn't true. Something had changed over the past two days. His actions toward her weren't those of a man trying to salvage a career. He cared what happened to her. And he believed, at least on some level, that she was innocent, or that she might be.

Following her accusation, the anger seeped out of him. "You don't really believe that, do you?"

She shook her head, ashamed of herself, mortified that her eyes were filling with tears.

"God, Wendy, when I think what could have happened . . ."

They both fell silent and simply looked at each other. Wendy felt the moment was frozen in time. She wished it would go on forever, that silent communion. She thought she was looking into his soul, and it was naked and bruised and vulnerable.

Either he was going to kiss her, or he was going to come to his senses and push her away. Wendy decided she didn't want the latter. Taking the choice away from him, she cradled his face between her hands and stood on tiptoe, touching her lips to his.

She was tentative at first, afraid he would reject her. Her breath caught in her throat at the feel of his firm, still mouth against hers. But it took only a moment for him to respond with blast-furnace heat. He took command of the kiss, angling his mouth against hers, his sudden desperation provoking her to match it.

Suddenly every one of her senses expanded to hypersensitivity. She could hear the traffic outside and the sound of Michael's breathing, like that of a racehorse after crossing the finish line. His well-washed cotton shirt was smooth against her hands when she ran them along his arms; the rasp of his beard was rough on the tender skin of her face. She smelled the new paint mixed with the unique scent of Michael, which reminded her of something from her past—high school proms and nerves. And the way he tasted—like pure sin.

The only sense that wasn't awakened was sight, because she had her eyes tightly closed, savoring all the rest. Surely no kiss had ever transported her the way this one did.

Michael's arms slid around her, holding her a willing prisoner. She felt safe from danger when he held her this way. Nothing outside could harm her. But who or what could protect her from him, and from her own crazy self?

She wasn't sure how or when they decided to make love, but neither one of them made even the slightest move toward stopping. There was no hesitation as one kiss turned into many, one caress flowed smoothly into another.

She didn't care that they stood in the entrance hall without even a carpet to lie on, thanks to her redecorating efforts. She didn't flinch when he reached under her shirt to touch her breasts through her whisper-thin bra. She didn't feel shy or embarrassed when he worked frantically at the buttons of her crisp work shirt until he'd freed her of the cumbersome garment. And she felt nothing but awe when he began stripping his own clothes off.

Oh, Lord, he had a beautiful body, all planes and angles, not a square inch of anything soft on it. He seemed bigger, somehow, after shedding his shirt, filling the room, overwhelming her senses.

She didn't wait for him to finish undressing her.

She shucked her jeans and socks in a heartbeat, watching his face as she did, watching his dark, deep eyes.

The hunger she saw in his expression fascinated her. She was positive no man had ever looked at her that way before, as if she were the most gorgeous creature on earth.

Michael paused as he reached for his belt buckle. "If you're going to stop this insanity, do it now," he said, his voice hardly more than a hoarse whisper.

She wouldn't dream of it, and started to say so. But just then he dropped his jeans, and no words came. She shook her head emphatically. Right or wrong, the heat of the moment ruled. Hesitation was for wimps. Regrets could wait till another day. She, Wendy Thayer, felt more alive than she had at any previous moment in her life, and she was taking full advantage of it.

When they were both naked, they stood and stared at each other once again. Now Wendy was the one who couldn't get enough breath, gasping loud enough to scare a paramedic.

She thought she would die before he touched her, and then he did so with such gentleness, such respect, that her heart came near to shattering. Where was her tough cop now?

"Come to me," he said. "Seeing you safe and sound isn't enough. I need more proof."

She understood. Dealing with death and danger on a daily basis, as she imagined he did, must make it doubly important for him to reaffirm life any way he could, as strongly as he could. She wouldn't have understood that concept a few days before, but at this moment she did. You couldn't be scared inside, she reasoned, while you were making love. And right now she needed not to be scared.

She took the two steps that closed the gap between them and pressed her body, naked skin to naked skin, against his. His arousal jutted against her abdomen, reminding her how virile a man he was. At any other time, his sex might have intimidated her, but not here, not now. She wiggled, deliberately rubbing herself against him, and he groaned in response.

She imagined him scooping her in his arms then and taking her to bed, but it didn't happen that way. A low table against one wall of the entrance hall sported a tacky plastic flower arrangement, which Wendy hadn't gotten around to replacing. With one sweeping gesture Michael sent it flying. Then he lifted her and sat her on the edge of the table.

Oh, yeah, this was going to work, she caught herself thinking. Since when had she become such a wanton creature? But now was not the time for self-analysis. She parted her legs and pulled him against her, then squeezed his hips between her thighs. His shaft brushed against her femininity, and she gasped at the sparks of pleasure that shot through her body.

She was suddenly consumed with the need to have him inside her, to claim and be claimed by this magnificent male animal. She reached between their bodies and touched him, stroking gently at first as he accustomed himself to her, then more boldly.

Not that he needed any help. He was like steel covered in velvet. She started to guide him home.

"You can't be ready . . ." he started to stay, but she nodded.

"Oh, yes, I can." She barely recognized the sultry, throaty voice coming out of her mouth.

As he slid inside her, it became obvious that she was more than ready. She was literally hot for him, and he filled her in one swift stroke. It was almost too perfect, and she cried out with sheer joy.

He didn't move at first, letting her get used to the feel of him inside her. She closed her eyes and threw her head back, letting her hair cascade down her bare back. When he did move, she found herself making strange, involuntary noises like some untamed creature from the jungle.

Her vocalizations seemed to excite Michael. He began moving, slowly at first, then faster, grasping her buttocks to pull himself even more deeply inside her. The most exquisite pressure built inside her, bringing tears to her eyes and a thickness to her throat. It wasn't just the physical sensations, she realized through her sensual haze. This was Michael, who was both her adversary and her champion, her devil and her angel. And at that moment she felt something very fierce and elemental, a possessiveness that bordered on insanity.

The moment she was waiting for came without warning, with no effort on her part. One moment she was floating along on a sea of indescribable pleasure, and the next she was drowning in it. Her cries echoed inside the little house, mixing with Michael's guttural noises as he lost control and emptied himself inside her.

She'd never experienced such a moment of joint exultation, as if they'd just won their own private Super Bowl.

Wendy wasn't sure what she expected him to say. She would have thought she'd be prepared for everything. But after they caught their breaths, while they were still clinging to each other, their bodies sheened with sweat, he shattered the mood.

"Wendy, please tell me you're on the Pill."

EIGHT

Michael knew it was the wrong thing to say the moment the words left his mouth. Of all the insensitive, boorish moves, asking about birth control *after the fact* had to be right up there at the top of the list.

Her mouth dropped open and she stared at him, her leaf green eyes blinking rapidly. Oh, Lord, he hadn't made her cry, he hoped.

He ran his fingers through her autumn-hued hair and caressed her cheek with one thumb. "That didn't come out the way I meant. It's just that normally I would think of that first, but you made me so crazy . . ." The Wendy Thayer Effect.

Her muscles relaxed. He could feel them loosening where her legs were wrapped around him, where his hand supported her bare back. "I'm not protected," she admitted.

Michael tried not to show panic, or any of the other myriad feelings stirring around inside him.

What if he had a child out of wedlock? What would that do to his plans, not to mention Wendy's?

But some traitorous part of his imagination took another tack. What would Wendy look like waddling around like Maggie Courtland? Would the baby have her auburn hair and green eyes?

Abruptly she turned those frightened eyes up to him. "Would they still make me go to jail if I'm pregnant?"

"Don't borrow trouble, Wendy. It was one time."

"Yeah, famous last words! What were we thinking? I've never done this, done *it* with no birth control, not ever."

He eased away from her, then turned and looked at the clothing-strewn entry hall. This had been a first in many ways for him. First time he'd ever done it on a hall table. With a suspect. And, yeah, with no protection. His father had drilled it into his head from the time he was thirteen—don't take chances, don't play Russian roulette with your DNA.

Looking back at Wendy, he wished he'd never brought up the subject, though she probably would have thought of it on her own before long. "Don't panic, please. On the infinitesimal chance that there are . . . consequences—"

"Don't call our baby 'consequences'!" she cried, hopping off the table. In one swift movement she scooped up her clothes and fled down the hall.

Michael stared after her, shaking his head. He'd just made love to a nut. He ought to regret it, the impulsiveness, the fact that he'd compromised his ethics all over the place. But he didn't. He found himself smiling as he put his own clothes back on.

He found Wendy in the bedroom, sitting against the scarred wooden headboard, fully clothed once again in a pale blue shirt and jeans. She had her knees pulled up and a pillow hugged to her chest.

"Can I come in?" he called softly.

She shrugged. "Sure."

He entered the humble room, where apparently Wendy's decorating urges hadn't yet penetrated. He sat on the edge of the bed, far enough away from her that he couldn't touch her if the urge struck him, which he was sure it would. Though not five minutes before, he'd satisfied himself with her to the nth degree, he still wanted to touch her.

She gave him a sheepish smile. "You must think I'm some kind of nutcase."

"The thought never crossed my mind," he lied.

"I need to explain something. You know how some women, when they have an orgasm, they laugh or cry, or scream or fall unconscious or whatever?"

"Yeah . . ." He wondered where *this* was going.

"Well, I get emotional. Whatever I happen to be feeling gets magnified a hundred times."

"Is this your cute little way of telling me you might have overreacted a minute ago?"

She cracked a smile, which for some reason filled Michael with relief. "Yeah. I get all illogical. Then it passes. Everything happened so quickly, I didn't have a chance to warn you."

"It's all right. No harm done. And, believe me, I

won't ever refer to little what's-its-name as 'Consequences' again. That would be a tough name to have to go through life with."

"Michael!" She threw the pillow at him, which he neatly dodged. It sailed past him to the floor, and he leaned over and snagged it.

"Wanna play rough?"

She grabbed the other pillow and held it in front of her like a shield, actually laughing. "No, no, I quit, uncle."

The playful mood deserted her as quickly as it had arrived. Wendy tossed the pillow aside. "You're right, there's no use worrying. But I think we should visit a drugstore immediately. Being caught unprepared once is one thing . . ." She let her voice trail off.

Damn. He hadn't wanted to have to make this speech. He'd thought for sure Wendy would be the first to start hollering about what a terrible mistake they'd made and they should never, *ever* repeat it. But apparently she didn't view their recent indiscretion as a one-time thing.

The possibilities shimmered between them like an electric current, tantalizing. He started to formulate a rationalization before he stopped himself.

"Wendy, we can't . . ." He ran his fingers through his thick, wavy hair, which hadn't seen a comb in too long. "What I mean is, I've got more to worry about than an unplanned pregnancy. You have to realize that I didn't just cross the line here, I jumped over it and stomped around."

"Oh." She cast her eyes down. He wished she

would look at him. He didn't want to hurt her feelings. "I guess this was sort of one of those wham-bam-thank-you-ma'am kind of things, huh?"

She made their lovemaking sound cheap and casual, which it hadn't been. But how could he explain?

He stood up and paced the small room, then started another explanation. "I've always been a good cop. My record is spotless. But this falls into the category of abusing my power, my authority, as a peace officer."

"Oh, baloney," she said flatly, scowling at him. "You didn't abuse anything. What just happened out there had nothing to do with you being a cop and me being a suspect. Unless you thought I might confess in the heat of the moment."

"No, I certainly wasn't thinking about the case," he said, unable to suppress an evil grin. When he'd been inside Wendy, he'd thought of nothing but her heat and her passion and his need to possess her completely.

"So what's the big deal?"

"The big deal is, if anyone found out about this, my application to the Bureau would get kicked back so fast, my head would spin. Hell, I might even lose my job. No, make that a certainty."

"And how, pray tell, would anyone find out about our making love?" she asked succinctly. "You think I'm going to call a press conference?"

He scratched his head. Didn't she get it? "Wendy, I wouldn't blame you if you did. You could probably get your whole case thrown out."

"Really?"

He didn't know why he was telling her this. He might as well call the damn press conference himself and sign a written confession. "Really."

"Well, I'll keep that in mind if the case should actually go to trial," she said with a toss of her head. Then she grew serious. "Michael, I'm not going to tell anyone. I don't believe in using sex as a weapon. I'll beat these charges against me with honesty and good old-fashioned detective work, not sleazy legal tricks."

Michael couldn't believe what he was hearing. He'd long ago given up on that kind of integrity. It seemed as if everyone he knew, everyone he dealt with, was out to beat the system and screw whoever it took to win.

Later he would realize that that was the moment he'd started to fall in love with Wendy Thayer.

"Thank you," was all he could think of to say.

"Now that we've got that out of the way, if you want to walk away from a night of indescribable pleasures, don't do it because you think it'll derail your career."

She was a tricky one, all right. She'd just argued him out of all his sensible reasons why they should forget about getting naked ever again.

"I can't offer you any promises," he said. "As soon as I'm accepted at the Bureau, I'll be shipping out to Quantico for training, then to Washington."

She thrust her chin out in a gesture he was becoming very familiar with. "I'm not looking for a long-term relationship," she said. "I just got rid of one boyfriend, and I'm not keen on finding a replacement any time soon. But I'm scared and feeling all alone, and you're real and warm and solid, and I just . . . I just need you tonight. Stay here with me. One night."

One night. A promise of eight or ten or twelve hours of incredible delight. "And then we both walk away?"

"Do we have any other choice?"

"No." But maybe, he thought, if he indulged every fantasy he'd had about Wendy—and he'd entertained plenty—he could get over his fixation on her.

"Make up your mind," she said, crossing her arms. "I don't make this sort of offer every day."

Ah, hell, he already knew what his answer was. No jury—provided it included plenty of heterosexual men—would ever convict him.

"You drive a hard bargain, lady," he said, reaching for her. "But if you're lonely, you're lonely, and I guess it's my job to remedy that."

Her eyes flared with remembered passion as he drew closer, intending to claim a kiss to seal the devil's bargain they'd just made. But she turned her head at the last moment. "Wait a minute. Condoms? Surely you aren't going to forget that."

No, he hadn't forgotten. "Sweets, I can think of lots and *lots* of things we can do that won't put you at risk. I bet you could think of some, too, if you put your mind to it."

"Ooooh." She grasped his collar with both hands and closed the distance between them. As they shared a searing kiss, Michael was amazed that his passion could be aroused again so quickly.

"By the way," she murmured in his ear, "how was your day?"

"If you *ever* make me get near those Poms again . . ." He couldn't think of a threat dire enough, so he kissed her again.

Hunger drove them from the warm, cozy, but sagging bed shortly after midnight.

"I'd feel better if you stayed here," Michael said as he donned his shirt. "I'll make a pizza-and-condom run."

In truth, Wendy was scared to stay alone. She didn't know how she'd done it the previous night. But it would probably be more dangerous to run around in the streets after midnight.

"All right," she agreed. "But hurry."

"I'll call the pizza in first. There's a place over on Hampton that stays open for pick-up all night long."

She propped herself up on the pillows and watched him dress, amazed at how close she felt to him. In the past few hours they'd explored each other's anatomies with the dedication of naturalists studying a new species. No area of her body had been overlooked or ignored, including her earlobes and the backs of her knees.

She tingled all over at the memory of Michael's bold caresses and the creative ways he'd thought of to share pleasure without actually making love. She'd found herself doing things she'd only dreamed of, or read about, and becoming an instant expert. Michael was an excellent teacher and a bright pupil.

They had so many lessons to teach each other. But morning would come too soon—what, in six or seven hours? Much as she'd like to stay up all night and indulge, they needed to get some sleep. Michael had to work the following day—his real job, not hers—and she absolutely would not be responsible for putting him out on the mean streets in a sleep-deprived haze.

"Back in a few," he whispered, grazing her forehead with his lips. "Don't move."

When he came back about thirty minutes later, she'd fallen asleep. The smell of pepperoni woke her, though. She was famished, having skipped both lunch and dinner. In the most decadent fashion they sprawled on the bed to eat their feast.

Wendy suddenly realized that they'd exchanged little conversation during the last few hours, other than "Mmm, that feels good," and "Don't stop."

"So, what do you really think of the redecorating?" she asked, trying to tell herself that his answer didn't mean anything to her. But she'd put a lot of herself into the overhaul. It would hurt her feelings if he hated it.

"That depends," he said, popping a mushroom slice into his mouth and chewing thoughtfully. "How much will it cost me?"

"Oh, that's the best part," she said, immediately waxing enthusiastic. The only thing she loved more than a bargain was bragging about it. "The whole thing only cost seventy-eight dollars, or thereabouts."

"You're kidding."

"No. Fabric-a-rama was having this incredible sale—I did all the curtains with remnants. The hardware store gave me a break on the paint because it was a custom color someone had returned. I kept the receipts for the rugs and pillows and throws. You can return or exchange those—"

"Oh, no, they're fine. I wouldn't dare tamper with the look."

"You're making fun of me."

His dark eyes twinkled. "No. I think you're dynamite. Next I'm going to turn you loose on my own house."

Wendy was inordinately pleased. He couldn't have said anything nicer. And the idea of infiltrating the lion's den, of spending time in his private home, selecting sheets and towels and all of the things he would live intimately with, sent a guilty thrill zinging up her spine.

"They say a good decorating job can make a huge difference in the sale price of a home," Michael mused. "I've talked to a real estate agent about listing my house, and she hinted that it needed a face-lift if I wanted to get my equity out of it."

Wendy's fantasy fell to earth with a thump. He wanted her to spiff up his house so he could sell it and move to Washington. She would do well to remember that.

They did a creditable job on the pizza, leaving only

two slices. Wendy, shamelessly naked, carried the leavings into the kitchen, storing the leftovers in the fridge and pitching the rest.

When she returned to the bedroom, to her delight she found Michael as bare as she, lounging across the bed like a big, lazy tom cat.

"Now, where were we before hunger struck?" He held up an obscenely long string of shiny plastic squares.

"Planning a busy night, are you?" she said, easing herself onto the bed next to him. She stroked one fingernail along his firm chest.

He dropped the condom packages and reached for her. "As busy as I can manage."

Wendy awoke before Michael the next morning. He was sprawled next to her, one possessive arm thrown across her chest, sleeping the sleep of the well satisfied.

In repose his face was relaxed, unlined, more boyish. His hair, normally on the unruly side, was positively rakish, and the shadow of beard darkening his face gave him a bad-boy look that made her heart beat faster.

He's not yours to keep, she told herself over and over. They'd been living on borrowed time, stealing those hours of reckless abandon. But with morning, sanity returned.

She had a life to return to, a business, a criminal case against her to defend. She had an appointment with Nathaniel, she remembered, to talk over the new charges against her and try to punch holes in the cops' allegations.

And, Lord, the mayor's party was the following day. She had to get hopping.

She knew darn well Michael would fight her tooth and nail about leaving his rental house and returning to work. But what if they never caught the person who was trying to hurt her? She couldn't live in fear the rest of her life. She wouldn't have a life to go back to if she didn't give her work more attention.

Then there were Bill and Ted. They had a continuous feeding machine and plenty of water, but they needed her affection, not to mention her skills in cleaning the litter box. Suddenly she missed her silly cats. She missed the normal routine, the occasional moments of boredom, the inconsequential worries—bills, keeping good personnel, advertising, watering her plants.

She looked at Michael again, her heart aching. The longer she lay there staring at him, wishing for things that would never be, the harder it would be to end their excruciatingly brief affair. She'd better just get on with her life.

With a sigh she got out of bed and dragged herself to the shower.

Wendy let the hot needles of water massage her aching muscles. She'd gotten an unaccustomed workout last night. Michael had challenged her creativity, not to mention her flexibility. She was sore in places that should never get sore. For days to come, her body would remind her of the previous night's pleasures. That was both a blessing and a curse.

After her shower she dressed in day-before-yesterday's clothes, which she'd managed to wash and dry. She combed out her hair. Every stroke reminded her of how Michael's fingers had felt combing through the tangled strands. She had a sad feeling that everything in the world—a color, pizza, the smell of new paint—would forever after remind her of Michael.

Had she made a mistake giving in to her temptation?

No. She wouldn't trade what they'd shared for anything.

She went into the kitchen to make a few phone calls. She needed to get back to her life, but she intended to take a few precautions.

Jillian, tapping into the office computer from home, gave Wendy a long list of tasks, including several things Michael hadn't gotten to.

"Where did you find that guy?" Jillian asked. "He's gorgeous, but I'm not sure he's suited to this kind of work."

"Don't worry, yesterday was his first and only day working for me. It was a temporary deal," Wendy explained breezily.

"Okay," Jillian said, indicating by her tone of voice that she didn't understand at all. "Now explain to me why you're not coming in today."

"Someone's been following me," Wendy said carefully, still reticent to reveal all the details. "I've shaken him for the moment, but I don't want to show up at places where he can catch up with me again. Which reminds me, could you run to my apartment during lunch, pick up my mail, and check on Bill and Ted?"

"Sure, but . . . Wendy, where are you?"

"Gotta go, bye!" She hung up, knowing that sooner or later she would have to fess up to her life of high adventure.

When she returned to the bedroom, Michael was just waking up. He surveyed her drowsily. "Whatcha doing?"

"Getting up. Moving around. Thinking about breakfast."

"You're a perky morning person, aren't you?" he accused.

"Yup."

"I'm not."

"I can see that." She smiled. God, he was damn near irresistible. But resist him she must. She couldn't afford to get any more stuck on the guy than she already was.

"Give me a minute," he said, rubbing his eyes. "Did you use all the hot water?"

"If you're looking for an excuse to stay in bed, I'm not giving it to you," she said crisply. "There's plenty of hot water left."

"Darn." He sat up and swung his legs over the side of the bed. "Did you say breakfast? Is there anything here to eat?"

"Yogurt."

He made a face of extreme distaste. "I'm taking

you out to Irene's Diner. Give me ten minutes, tops."
He headed for the bathroom.

Her heart ached. She'd already called her taxi. It
would be there any minute. This was the coward's way
out, but she knew that if Michael discovered her plans,
he would talk her out of them. She was no good at
resisting that man's will.

Michael didn't have anyone to curse at, so he
cursed at the hapless deejay on his car radio as he
drove to the station. How could he have been so careless as to let Wendy escape? How could he have been
so unobservant that he didn't see the signs that she was
going to leave him?

Now she was out running around, God knew
where, exposing herself to all kinds of danger. If she
got herself killed, it wouldn't look very good on his
résumé.

Michael put a stop to that line of thinking. This
really had nothing to do with his career. He was roy-
ally ticked because she'd been his lover and she'd
walked out. He was the one who'd put the limits on
their relationship. He was the one calling the shots. To
have her suddenly taking control rubbed him the
wrong way, particularly because he cared.

Any other suspect, he'd be saying to hell with it.
You want to put yourself in danger despite all my best
advice, then knock yourself out. Save the taxpayers the
cost of your trial.

But it didn't work that way with Wendy. The

thought of her getting herself iced paralyzed him with fear and wracked him with guilt. Why hadn't he gotten through to her? Why hadn't he made the situation more clear? Why the hell did he care so much what happened to her?

When he walked into the squad room, a couple of catcalls and whistles greeted him. Full of trepidation, he went directly to Joe's desk. His partner was on the phone, but he flashed Michael a thumb's-up sign, then pointed to Michael's desk next door. That's when he saw the pink message slip.

In two strides he was at his desk. He snatched the small piece of paper off the desk's messy surface and read it, then groaned.

The message was from Wendy: *Don't worry about me, I'm fine, and the baby is fine.*

"All right," he said to the room in general, "who took this message?"

"I did," Joe said with a shrug. "That's exactly what she said."

"She must be talking about Maggie," Michael murmured. It was much too early to know anything about little Consequences. Wendy had probably just wanted to let him know that despite their lack of expertise in the field of obstetrics, they'd done the Courtland baby no irreparable harm. His irritation receded as he remembered the incredible experience of bringing a child into the world.

When he looked up, he realized half the guys in the squad room were watching him, and he had a goofy smile on his face. "It's not mine," he said succinctly.

"Yeah, that's what they all say," someone called out.

Michael shook his head and tossed the message into the trash can. Wendy.

Joe came over and propped one hip on Michael's desk. "So, what's the story, Tagg?"

"There is no story," Michael said, trying to make sense of the mess on his desk. Even one day away from his work caused things to stack up. Piles of messages, memos, things he was supposed to read and pass on—

"So where were you yesterday? You were pretty mysterious when you called."

"It was my day off." Michael didn't look up at his partner. He hated it when Joe got chatty.

"Thought you were gonna put in some overtime. It got pretty lonely here."

"I had things to do, okay?" Michael sighed. "It's just this art deco case . . . it's got my brains scrambled." He knew it was a lame excuse for snapping at Joe, who was the nicest guy in the world.

"I tried calling you last night, but you weren't home."

Michael didn't rise to that bait.

"Not last night . . . not at three o'clock in the morning, either."

Michael nearly rose out of his chair. "What were you doing calling me at three o'clock in the morning?"

"Checking up on you," Joe said affably. "If you got

a new squeeze, just tell me. I won't be monopolizing your time."

"Jeez, Joe, you sound like a jealous fishwife. Knock it off. You want me to apologize for not giving you my itinerary, or what?"

"So who is she?"

Michael could see he wasn't going to sidestep this one easily. He and Joe had worked together a long time. He couldn't lie to his friend, and he couldn't dismiss him with a curt "None of your business," either.

"I was protecting our suspect," he said, looking up at Joe with narrowed eyes, daring him to challenge the explanation. "In case it slipped your attention, she was almost murdered yesterday. Twice. And since the great police department can't spare even one man to keep an eye on her, I did it myself."

"Holy . . ." Joe let out a low whistle. "I knew you had a thing for this babe, but—"

"I do not have a 'thing' for her. I just don't want her killed before we find out what the truth is."

"A few days ago you knew the truth. She was guilty and that was that. I never knew you to be swayed by a pair of legs before."

That was when Michael realized Joe was deliberately trying to get a rise out of him. "My opinion has changed because of newly revealed evidence," Michael said, keeping his voice calm and deliberate—and hoping desperately that what Joe accused him of wasn't true.

"Oh, speaking of new evidence . . ." Joe returned

to his own desk and came back with another message slip. Suddenly he was all business again. Apparently he'd tired of getting his laughs at Michael's expense. "The lady from the bank called just a few minutes ago. Amazingly, she does remember Bernard Neff from when he opened his account."

"How can that be?" Michael asked, his mind back on the case. "It was over six months ago. Like Wendy said, the bank employee must have opened a hundred accounts since then."

"According to the bank services lady, this guy was memorable," Joe said.

"Oxygen tank?" Michael asked hopefully. "Arthritis? Gold tooth?"

Joe was shaking his head. "The customer in question was in his early thirties and very good-looking."

Michael's heart sank. Here, finally, was evidence that directly contradicted Wendy's story.

"I hate to bring this up, but does Ms. Thayer have a boyfriend?"

Michael nodded. "Ex-boyfriend, according to her. Recent breakup." He hated to even consider the possibility, but Wendy's boyfriend dumping her had occurred at a coincidentally convenient time. If he was the burglar, he might have set her up to take the fall.

Michael supposed he was ethically obligated to track down James Batliner and make him sweat. And if the idiot was innocent, if he'd had nothing to do with the art deco heist, Michael still intended to make him uncomfortable. Just for the hell of it.

NINE

Michael detested James Batliner on sight. Wendy's exboyfriend was an account executive with a large ad agency, and he was everything Michael was not, and nothing Michael wanted to be—blond, blue-eyed, movie-star handsome, and dressed as if he'd just walked off the pages of *GQ*. And he was stupid. Not obviously so, Michael conceded. But he must have been, to dump Wendy.

"The first I heard about Wendy's troubles is when I read about it in the paper yesterday," James said, shaking his head sadly. The two men were in an overdecorated conference room at James's office. Rather than being embarrassed or worried that a cop wanted to question him, he seemed to enjoy the drama.

"You were close to her over the last few months, closer than anyone else, probably," Michael remarked. "Did you notice any behavior that seemed . . . peculiar? Unexplained late-night absences, secretiveness?"

He focused his questions on Wendy rather than implying that he thought James might have something to do with the burglaries or the jewel-and-art heist. He didn't want to put his new quarry on the defensive too early.

"Well . . . nothing obvious. She did start spending money like crazy."

"Spending money?" Michael repeated. "On what?"

"The new office, for one thing. Hiring new employees. New company van. And advertising. I did the ads for her."

"I'll bet she got a good deal too," Michael murmured as he made notes, figuring Wendy was too savvy to pay full price for anything.

This information about the shopping was nothing new to Michael. Wendy had already explained about her expansion plans and how she was carrying them out. He was relieved James didn't mention anything about trips to Rio or new Cadillacs.

"I got her the best cable TV deal you can imagine. Anyway, other than that, I can't think of anything unusual in her behavior." James paused, pulling on his earlobe, his forehead crinkling with what might pass for deep thought. "Frankly, it doesn't surprise me that Wendy has run afoul of the law. It's in her genes, I guess."

Michael looked up sharply. "Excuse me?"

"You know, her father."

Wendy's father was deceased. She'd told him so herself.

"Ah, I can see I've surprised you. Wendy doesn't mention her father to everyone. Or she tells people he died. But he's been in and out of jail since Wendy was a kid. Last I heard, it was ten-to-twenty in Leaven-worth for wire fraud."

Michael made a show of writing this information down, hoping to hide his roiling emotions. It wasn't that he was horribly shocked that Wendy's father was a habitual criminal, if what James had told him was true. It was that she hadn't trusted him with the infor-mation. She'd lied to him. Even after all they'd been through, she hadn't come clean.

"Kinda makes you wonder what else she's misled you about," James said. "Don't you think?"

Though Michael was thinking that very thing him-self, it took all of his self-control not to wipe that stu-pid, smug grin off James's face with, say, a chair.

He settled for the next best thing. "Let me ask you one more thing, Mr. Batliner. Can you account for your whereabouts on these evenings?" He handed James a preprinted list of the dates of the home break-ins and the museum heist. "Wendy had an accomplice who meets your description," he added almost casu-ally. And James did resemble the "Bernard Neff" de-scribed by the new-accounts woman at the bank.

James blinked a couple of times, then looked up. Michael enjoyed the expression of consternation on his face. "Are you insinuating that I had something to do with Wendy's crime spree?"

"I'm just asking a question."

"I resent the implication."

"Resent all you want. I'd still like an answer."

James's face turned red, and he tugged at his perfectly knotted silk tie. "These dates go back almost six months. It will take me some time to check over my calendar."

"I'll call you tomorrow, then. That enough time?"

James nodded sharply. "That should do."

Michael was relieved to be back out in the sunshine, away from the rigid, oppressively corporate world of James's ad agency. What had Wendy ever seen in that guy, besides money and good looks? And how, Michael caught himself thinking, did he himself compare in her eyes?

Stupid to let it enter his mind, he thought as he climbed into his loaner car from the motor pool, an aging Chevy Lumina with almost two hundred thousand miles. He and Wendy were a done deal. Except . . . he had a few more questions for her. He'd also like to know if she was safe, if she was taking precautions. She'd willingly walked away from his efforts to protect her, but his gut still clenched at the thought of any danger befalling her.

Michael pulled his cellular out of his pocket and dialed her work number.

"Born to Shop, this is Jillian, may I help you?"

"Yes. I need to speak to Wendy, please."

"Is this Michael Taggert?" Jillian asked suspiciously.

"Yeah," He refrained from adding, *What about it?*

"Wendy told me you're a cop," Jillian huffed.

"Really, how could you arrest her? You police are just so incompetent! What a totally ridiculous notion—"

"Is she there?" Michael asked, breaking into Jillian's tirade. "If she's there, she's not safe."

"We're keeping the door locked."

That was a small relief. A lock might slow down a hit man long enough so they could call 9-1-1. "Then she is there."

A pause. "She's not taking phone calls."

"She has to talk to me," he said, pulling rank. "She's out on bail, and a condition of that bail is that she make herself available for police questioning."

Another pause, longer this time. The next voice he heard was Wendy's. "H-hi, Michael."

He wasn't prepared for what the sound of her voice did to him. His heart accelerated, his ears started ringing, and he suddenly remembered what her voice had sounded like in the throes of passion.

"Michael?" she said again when he didn't respond.

"Wendy." His own voice sounded rough. "I need to talk to you."

"Okay. You're not mad, are you?"

Mad didn't begin to describe the way he'd felt when he'd come out of the shower to find Wendy gone. Furious was closer. Betrayed. Pole-axed. Broadsided.

He pulled to the side of the road, afraid he'd have a wreck if he tried to drive in Dallas traffic when he was so distracted. "Let me just put it this way," he said. It was easier to clothe his myriad feelings in anger rather than try to sort out how he really felt about Wendy.

"If you give me even the slightest reason, I'll go to the judge and get your bail revoked."

"Okay, you're mad." At least she had the good grace to sound remorseful. "That's established. But I had to—I couldn't face—I just had to get back to work, and I knew you'd try to stop me."

"Damn straight. Do you have any idea—"

"Of course I know the danger I'm in," she said. "But I can't let these stupid criminal charges and these horrible people destroy my business."

Michael hadn't been about to remind her of the danger. He'd been about to ask her if she had any idea how he'd felt when he'd come out of the shower to find himself alone. As if he'd been kicked in the gut by a bucking bronco. But apparently Wendy's business was more important than a mere personal involvement.

Ah, hell, he was thinking like a teenager who'd been stood up for the prom. She was right. Her physical safety was the crucial thing.

"You realize," he said, "that by hanging out at your office, you're putting other people besides yourself in jeopardy."

"I know. And I told Jillian she could take the day off, but she wouldn't. There's a cop who regularly patrols this area. I explained the situation to him and he's keeping an especially close eye on the office today. I'm being as careful as I know how to be."

Michael took a deep breath. He'd still feel better if she were under lock and key, but he supposed she was taking reasonable precautions. He didn't believe Mr.

Neff or his associates would bust through the front door to kill her. They couldn't afford to get caught.

"Fine. I still need to ask you some questions. Is now a good time?" He didn't really care if it was convenient or not. He was coming over.

"Any time," she said, her tone cool. "I'll be here."

Wendy paced the office nervously while she waited for Michael to get there. She was having second thoughts about how she'd left him that morning. She'd told herself it was the only way she could take back control of her life. But now her actions struck her as a tad mean-spirited.

Michael had given her the most incredible night of sexual pleasure imaginable. The next morning he hadn't turned cold and distant, the way some men did when they wanted to make it clear they weren't involved. Instead he'd talked about taking her out for a nice breakfast. But something inside her had balked at the idea.

Was that when he would tell her that, nice as it was, their brief dalliance was over? In a public place where she couldn't cry or make a scene?

She'd left him to emerge from the shower to find himself all alone because she hadn't wanted him to say the words severing the personal angle of their relationship. She'd wanted to do the severing.

Well, she'd done it, all right. On the phone he'd sounded as if he wanted to hang her on a clothesline and let crows peck at her. If there'd been any chance for a lasting—

But there wasn't, she reminded herself. Aside from the impropriety of their dalliance, they could hardly carry on a meaningful relationship when he was in Washington and she was in Dallas.

Still, the FBI might reject Michael's application. And at some point she would be free of these criminal charges. Then, maybe, just maybe . . .

Oh, why was she doing this to herself? Who was to say she was anything more than a quick, convenient tumble for him? He'd *said* that he'd never compromised himself with a suspect, but did she really know that was true? Her father had been a lawman, and look how dishonest he was.

She flopped into a chair, miserable. Michael was a good man, a conscientious cop, and nothing like her father. She believed him. He'd been more than fair with her, and she'd treated him abominably.

"You got a thing for this cop?" Jillian asked.

"No!" Wendy answered too quickly.

"You're awfully worked up." Jillian smiled. "Lord knows he's handsome enough. I wouldn't blame you."

"He said he wanted to question me." Wendy picked up a paper clip from the desk and started mangling it. "That means he has some new information. I'm nervous, that's all." It was partly true.

He arrived sooner than she would have liked, before she was ready. The glass door was locked. Michael tapped on it, and Jillian grabbed her purse and scurried to the front with the key.

"I'm going to the Taco Plaza for lunch," she announced. "I'll bring you back something." She gave Michael a hard look as she let him inside, then slipped out.

"I've got a coupon for Taco Plaza," Wendy called after her, but Jillian was already locking the door behind her.

Wendy wished her office manager had stayed. She didn't want to face Michael alone. He looked as dark and forbidding as he had the first time she'd seen him, when he'd approached her at the bank with the handcuffs.

She opened her mouth, about to issue some kind of greeting, when the phone rang. She held up one finger, indicating she'd be only a minute, and picked up the phone on Jillian's desk.

"Born to Shop, this is Wendy."

It was the caterer working on the mayor's party.

"Yes, that's right, we've upped the guest list to 210. And Mrs. Munn has changed her mind about the shrimp canapés. She wants liver pâté instead. Oh, by the way, Sellman's Meat Market has the best . . . you already knew that. Okay. I'll confirm everything with you tomorrow."

"Still working on the mayor's party?" Michael asked, swiveling a chair around and straddling it.

She nodded. "Mrs. Munn is standing behind me a hundred percent. A lot of my other clients are on the guest list. If they see that the Munns still trust me, maybe they will too. I have to make sure I don't mess anything up, either. I still have to make last-minute

arrangements with the florist, the valet-parking atten-
dants, security . . ." She realized she was rambling.

She sank into Jillian's chair. "So, let's have it.
What do you need to know?"

"It's about James Batliner."

Wendy's heart sank. She didn't owe James anything, but she'd been hoping to shield him from the
investigation. His employer was so uptight, he might
suffer repercussions if her legal troubles spilled over
onto him. "What about him?"

"Did his behavior change in the past six months?
Any unexplained absences, sudden show of wealth, se-
cretive behavior?"

"You think James might be Mr. Neff?" Wendy
laughed. That was ludicrous.

"I think he might be Mr. Neff's accomplice. A man
meeting your lover-boy's description opened Mr.
Neff's bank account."

She sobered immediately. Was it possible? She
tried to give Michael's question serious consideration.
"He did have a pretty flashy lifestyle," she said.
"Drove a Porsche, wore Italian suits, that kind of
thing. But his family has money. Lots of it. There's no
way his salary could support his habits, but I always
assumed he had a trust fund or something."

"Did he have access to your computer?"

She nodded. "He liked to play games on it. Sometimes he would start some space war game and play it
till three or four in the morning."

"So he used your computer for long periods of
time without your monitoring him?"

"Well, yeah. But my work files were password protected, and I never told him my password. There was no reason to."

"Wendy, *I* know your password. You should never use something as easy as your birthday."

She stared at him in stunned silence. "How did you—"

"It doesn't matter. Anyone could have broken into your files. Which means there are lots of potential suspects now."

Wendy shook her head vehemently. "Not my staff. Not them. Don't you dare question them." They were so good, so loyal. All of them had stood behind her when they'd found out about the accusations against her. They'd all volunteered to testify on her behalf as character witnesses.

"If not your staff or James, then who? If we don't come up with a viable alternative, the jury will convict you. Whoever engineered those burglaries got the security codes from your computer or your organizer, no doubt about it. Help me figure out who it is, or my hands are tied."

Wendy took a deep breath. She'd met with Nathaniel that morning, and he'd told her that her case looked grim. His private investigator hadn't turned up anything the police hadn't already found. If she didn't come up with the real guilty party, she was going to jail.

Was it remotely possible James was in on the crime? She'd like to believe she was a better judge of character. But she hadn't in a million years believed James was a philanderer, either, till he'd confessed.

"I feel like a real witch saying this," she said, "but I suppose James could be involved."

"Great," Michael said, warming to the idea. "Do you have a picture of him?"

She had to think a minute. "Wait." She went to the back of the office, to the cubbyhole where her desk was. There, in the drawer, she found some snapshots taken at James's family's Christmas party. There were a couple of pretty good ones of James. She pulled them out of the envelope and hurried back to Michael.

"Will these do?"

Michael studied them, and a strange expression came over his face. She thought for one breathtaking moment that he was going to kick something or tear the pictures up. Then he pressed his mouth into a grim line and stuck the snapshots into the inside pocket of his sport coat. "They'll do. Oh, Wendy. Your mother's still living, right?"

"Yes, but she's in Florida, thank God, where news of my arrest will never reach her, unless one of her nosy but well-meaning friends sends her the newspaper clipping. Why?"

"I'd like to talk to her."

A wave of panic washed over Wendy. "You can't!"

He flashed an almost predatory smile. "Afraid she'll contradict something you've told me?"

"No, no, it isn't that." Wendy and her mother had long ago gotten their stories straight regarding Wendy's father. Marcella Thayer wouldn't contradict her daughter. "It's just that if she finds out I've been arrested, she'll be very upset." Marcella would think Wendy was her father's Bad Seed. During all of Wendy's growing-up years her mother had watched her closely, worried that some of her ex-husband's aspects would manifest in their offspring when she wasn't looking.

"Any other family? You told me your father died when you were five. Does he have any relatives you're close to?"

Why this sudden interest in her family? she wondered. She supposed investigations into family background were normal and routine, but it made her nervous. Not that there was any way Michael could guess her father's true whereabouts. If he did, if he knew about it, he would have to include it in his report. And once the D.A. got hold of the fact that her father was a habitual criminal, she would be toast.

That's why she hadn't been truthful with Michael. She knew he would never lie for her.

"No, there's no one," she said.

Abruptly he got up and headed toward the door without even saying good-bye, though after he'd turned the dead bolt to let himself out, he ordered her to lock the door behind him.

Michael's heart ached as he sat at his desk later that afternoon, filling out a report on the Wendy Thayer case. He'd lost Wendy before he'd ever really had her in more than a purely physical sense, and there wasn't a damn thing he could do about it.

She'd lied to him. Looked him right in the eye and lied about her father. Michael had checked out James's story, of course. And there was, indeed, a Dickson Thayer in Leavenworth serving ten-to-twenty for wire fraud. If Wendy didn't trust him enough to confide a painful part of her past to him, then how could he trust her with the really important stuff?

It had taken him until now to realize how important she'd become to him. If he thought it would serve any useful purpose, he would go to his supervisor and request that the case be turned over to another detective, that he'd lost his objectivity. But he couldn't make himself do that. Another detective might not put the care into the investigation that Michael had. Another detective might look at the surface facts, assume Wendy was guilty, and ignore any leads that contradicted that conclusion.

He'd certainly followed every lead he could think of. He had an appointment the next morning with the bank employee. He intended to show her a photo lineup, mixing James's snapshot in with a few other handsome, fair-haired men in their thirties to see if she would pick him out.

But even if he succeeded in casting blame on James Batliner, that wouldn't get Wendy off the hook. She and James had been more than casual acquaintances. The easy intimacy between them had been obvious in one of the pictures Wendy had given him. James's arm had been casually slung around Wendy's shoulders.

And Wendy, looking delectable in a dark green velvet dress, her hair loose and curly around her face, had been looking at him with a smile of fondness and familiarity.

The picture had produced a visceral reaction in Michael, and it had been all he could do not to reveal how insanely jealous her past relationship with James made him feel.

A shadow fell across his desk. He looked up, and though he hadn't believed his heart could sink any lower, it did. Standing before him was Mayor Munn, and hizzonor wasn't smiling.

"Wendy hasn't been cleared yet," the mayor said succinctly. "That article in the paper could ruin her. And it will be on your conscience."

Michael steeled himself for the verbal battle he knew was coming. Munn had won the last election after a series of televised debates, during which he trounced his opponent with both logic and quick thinking.

"Ms. Thayer's arrest is a matter of public record," Michael said, telling himself to remain calm. "I have no control over what the press prints. But I did stress to the reporter who interviewed me that Ms. Thayer's guilt was not a foregone conclusion." His investigative work couldn't be faulted. He was confident he would have the right answers to the mayor's questions.

The mayor glared. "Maybe I didn't make myself understood. I want the woman cleared, and I want it done today. If you haven't found the evidence to do that, then you need to put in some overtime."

Michael was tired of his investigation being called into question. "Let me make *my*self clear," he said through gritted teeth. It was all he could do not to stand up and mirror the mayor's intimidating posture. "I am doing everything I know how to do. Would you like to review the file? Maybe you can find a lead I've missed, a piece of evidence I've overlooked. But I doubt it. Because I've spent more hours on this case than any other five cases I've ever worked, combined. I've interviewed dozens of witnesses, logged almost a hundred phone calls. And I don't appreciate some rich fat cat from city hall telling me I'm not doing my job, even if he is ex-FBI."

The entire squad room, he noticed, had gone unnaturally silent. Even the phones had stopped ringing.

Munn fairly vibrated with rage. "No one talks to me like that. I'll have your badge, Taggert." He swung on his heel and walked away as if he had a steel rod up his back.

As soon as the mayor was gone, a spotty round of applause broke out among the other detectives in Theft.

"Way to go, Tagg," Smythe called from his desk in a back corner. "Way to work those political connections."

Michael made a rude gesture toward his colleagues. "Y'all are just jealous 'cause I'll be out of this hellhole pretty soon," he said, pretending he wasn't disturbed by the mayor's threat. "I'll be working for a real law enforcement agency."

"Yeah, or you'll be in the unemployment line," Smythe said.

Michael ignored the good-natured ribbing and went back to his report. He wasn't altogether sure that Smythe was wrong. He suspected the mayor was mostly bluster, but what if he *could* exert enough influence to get Michael fired? If he nixed his appointment to the FBI, that was survivable. He still had a job, one that he was damn good at despite the lack of promotions, one he usually enjoyed despite the frustrations. Anyway, he wasn't feeling as confident about the Bureau anymore. His potential employers had been distressingly quiet this past week.

Joe wandered over to Michael's desk. "Hey, Tagg, you still planning on skipping the mayor's party? 'Cause it might be a chance for you to earn some major brownie points. I hear Munn's invited some of his former Fibbie colleagues."

"Hmm." Michael accompanied his noncommittal reply with a shrug. More than likely, the mayor would use his party as an opportunity to squeeze the vice a little tighter. Or embarrass him in front of his potential future employers.

"You know who's put the whole party together, right?" Joe asked with an unmistakable leer.

"Yeah." Wendy had been obsessing about this bash for days.

"Chatty, aren't you. Don't you want to see our little suspect in action?"

"I've seen her in action." Her presence at the party was his number one reason for wanting to skip the whole thing. He wouldn't have admitted it to anyone, but he was torn up about Wendy Thayer—about her lying, about her leaving him that morning, about the possibility of her going to jail. She'd twisted him up into so many knots, he didn't think he'd ever be the same.

The old man had never felt so frustrated. He couldn't leave the country until he had this little matter of Wendy Thayer tied up—otherwise he might not be able to come back. Did Tahiti have an extradition agreement with the United States?

But back to Wendy. She'd eluded his best man. She managed to slip around as easily as a shadow, shielding her whereabouts with an expertise that amazed him. And when he did know her location, she constantly surrounded herself with people, particularly cops, making it impossible for anyone to execute a clean hit.

He could see now that he'd made a mistake by not taking care of her himself. But he'd have another chance Saturday night. It wouldn't be hard to lure her away from the crowd. And though her death would be ruled a homicide, the police force would have a whole house full of suspects—hundreds of them—to contend with. He would be the last person they'd question.

TEN

The day of the mayor's party dawned clear and bright. Wendy got out of bed with renewed optimism. No one had tried to kill her in a couple of days. She'd even managed to wedge a video aerobics routine into her morning before the phone started ringing.

Wendy knew who it would be even before she picked up the receiver. Alice Munn was a dear lady, the aunt of one of Wendy's high school friends. She was a pleasure to work for and one of Born to Shop's best clients. But she was a worrywart, and she'd never thrown a party of this magnitude.

Neither had Wendy. But everything was in place.

"Wendy," Alice said, breathless. "I'm sorry to bother you at home, but where are the party favors? We have to have party favors."

"They're in the trunk of my rental car." As the guests departed, a footman would hand each one a small vial of rare perfume or a set of designer golf tees, depending on their sex.

"Are they wrapped?" Alice asked.

"The perfume is in silver netting, and the golf tees are in shiny black paper with a silver ribbon."

"Oh, that sounds divine. When will the caterers arrive?"

"Five o'clock. Same time as the florist."

"The sitter for the kids?"

"Six."

"The valets?"

"Seven. Your hair appointment is at one o'clock, and I'm picking up your dress from the alterations place at noon."

"The candles for the front walkway—"

"—should be arriving any minute. I'll light them myself. Mrs. Munn, try to relax. We don't want you to trigger an asthma attack. Oh, that reminds me, I picked up a new inhaler for you. I'll bring it when I bring the dress."

"Wendy, you're a gem. I couldn't do this without you. If there's anything I can do . . . you know, about the recent troubles you've been having . . ."

"Recent troubles" sounded more like a sinus infection than criminal charges. "Your husband has certainly done his part keeping the pressure on the police," Wendy said. "If you'll just let me leave some business cards stacked discreetly on a table in the entrance hall—"

"Not on your life. I'll personally hand a card to

everyone I talk to, and I'll make personal introductions to anyone you'd like to meet."

"Thank you, Mrs. Munn. Your support means everything to me." Well, not everything, she conceded silently as she hung up. There was a gaping hole in her heart where Michael's support had been. She deeply regretted turning away from him, and the lies she'd told him about her father practically burned a hole in her conscience. She'd left him the previous morning to save herself heartache later on.

But could she feel any worse than she felt now? She'd assumed he would take her abandonment in stride. But if he felt even a tenth the emotions that had staked out her heart, then he was hurting, and she ought to be ashamed of herself for treating him so shoddily.

If she had a spare minute, she would go to him and apologize, throw herself on his mercy. She might also come clean about her father. She would feel so much better.

The catch was, she didn't think she would have a spare minute. The tasks connected with the mayor's party would eat up every second of her time.

Tomorrow, then. Tomorrow was Sunday, traditionally her day off. Maybe Michael would have the day off too. She never had figured out exactly how his schedule worked. She could invite him over, cook him breakfast. They could go to White Rock Lake and walk the bike path, taking advantage of the incredible spring weather they were having. And they could clear the air.

By the time she realized she was staring into space, consumed with her outlandish fantasy of holding hands and feeding the ducks, she'd wasted five minutes. She had to feed Bill and Ted, then get to the office.

It seemed as if Michael was getting more than his share of dressing down lately. First the mayor, now his own superior, Captain Larry Rogers. Though Rogers was in general a fair man, he and Michael often did not see eye to eye.

"Do you have any idea who James Batliner's parents are?" Rogers demanded. They were in his office: Michael was sitting in a chair getting really hot under the collar, and Rogers was pacing.

"Yeah, so his parents are muckety-mucks."

"Major supporters of the city manager. And I don't need to remind you how important it is to have his support behind this department. You've already got the mayor pissed off at us."

"So, Captain, what am I supposed to do? Wendy Thayer's a friend of the mayor, so we forget prosecuting her. I come up with an alternate suspect, but it turns out he's a friend of the city manager's, so I sweep it under the rug. There's a name for that. Corruption."

"You don't have any real evidence against Batliner."

"The bank employee picked him out of a photo lineup."

"The lineup wasn't done under controlled conditions. It won't hold up in court."

"Only because you wouldn't let me bring Batliner in for a real lineup. He doesn't have a single alibi for any of the burglaries, including the museum."

"Tagg, *I* wouldn't have an alibi. The burglaries all occurred between two and three in the morning. Most people who live alone won't be able to account for their whereabouts during those hours because they're asleep. Alone."

Michael conceded the point. He probably wouldn't be able to come up with an alibi himself for those times. "So, I repeat, what do you want me to do? This guy, Batliner, is in up to his eyeballs. My gut tells me that, and you know my gut's never wrong."

The captain rubbed his forehead. "This has to be handled delicately. What about the physical evidence at the burglaries?"

"We've got a couple of partial fingerprints, a shoe print, one hair, and some teeth marks."

"Teeth marks?"

"Yeah, the burglar took a bite out of an apple at one house and left it sitting on the counter. If I could just haul Batliner in and take samples—"

"God, no! We'd be sued so fast, our heads would spin."

Michael thought for a minute. "What if I could get samples without him knowing?"

Rogers narrowed his eyes. "How do you propose to do that?"

"He's sure to be at the mayor's party, right?"

"I thought you weren't going."

"I changed my mind. I'll get something from him and we'll quietly compare it with the evidence. And if I get a match—"

"If you get a match, we'll go after him. I promise."

That was all Michael needed to hear.

Wendy had dressed with care in the only summery cocktail dress she owned, a sea-foam green designer number she'd snagged at a resale shop. The sheath fit her as if it had been tailored for her, draping sensuously down to her ankles. She'd purchased a pair of silvery spike-heeled sandals during the two-for-one sale at Vantage Shoe Warehouse, and Jillian had loaned her the coolest silver evening bag, shaped like an apple. As a final touch, she'd woven a silver beaded necklace into her hair, which she wore piled up on her head in a mass of curls and braids.

She'd decided it would be to her advantage to appear on a par with the guests, instead of dressing in a uniform like hired help, even though that's what she was. In evening wear she could wander about the mayor's mansion at will, discreetly checking the buffet for items that needed replenishing, making sure there were plenty of champagne flutes and silverware, adjusting the thermostats and stereo systems in various rooms to be certain the guests were comfortable and that the music wasn't too loud or too soft.

Alice Munn was actually the one who'd suggested that Wendy dress up. "You show those clients who turned their backs on you that you're one of *them,*" she'd said. "You've got more class in your little finger than some of those old biddies have in their whole bodies."

Wendy had laughed and given her best client a hug. Alice had never been one to judge someone based on income or family lineage.

Now that she was ready, Wendy was feeling a flutter of nerves. She'd checked every detail a dozen times. Nothing was going to go wrong. This party would be her calling card, her pièce de résistance.

She arrived at the Munns' posh estate at the same time as the caterers and florist.

"You look stunning, an absolute goddess," Alice raved. The diminutive mayor's wife was still in her bathrobe. "Are you still seeing the, um, Batliner boy? What's his name?"

"James. And no, James and I are no longer an item."

Alice frowned. "Not because of this police business, I hope."

"No, it happened before my arrest." Hours before, come to think of it. Could there be a connection? At first she'd thought Michael was crazy for thinking James was involved, but the more she'd thought about it, the more she'd started to wonder. He'd asked her out the first time just days after the date of the Art Deco Museum heist.

"He'll be here tonight, I believe," Alice said. "I hope that won't be uncomfortable for you."

Wendy smiled and shook her head. "Listen,

there'll be so many people here, I'll probably never see him." And if she did, she added silently, she looked so awesome that James's date—whoever she was—would seem a frump by comparison. She found that the mean-spirited thought gave her no pleasure at all. She really didn't care what James did.

She only cared about Michael, she realized with a painful thud of her heart. She'd fallen in love with him, crazy as that seemed. He'd started out as her nemesis, he'd become her champion, and now he was detached and impersonal. She would definitely prefer the verbal sparring that had marked their first day together to the coolness between them now.

At least she wouldn't have to worry about running into him at the party. Though he'd once worked under the guest of honor, the retiring Walt Patterson, he'd made it quite clear that froufrou parties weren't his thing.

"You'd better get dressed," Wendy said, patting Alice on the shoulder. "T minus forty-five minutes and counting."

The first guests started arriving at eight o'clock on the dot. Mr. and Mrs. Munn were there to greet them, resplendent in their formal attire. Champagne flowed, classical music drifted on the air, and the canapés started to disappear with heartening regularity. The crowd flowed from room to room, spilling out onto the patio as the number of guests increased steadily.

Wendy caught sight of James with a tall, cool blonde on his arm. The woman was more his style than she was, Wendy decided without even a twinge of regret. She intended to stay out of his way so there would be no need for any awkward conversation.

Alice caught up with her in the kitchen, where Wendy supervised the arrangement of a cheese tray destined for the library.

"Oh, Wendy, there you are. I hate to ask you this, because I know you're busy—"

"What is it, Mrs. Munn?" she asked pleasantly, steeling herself for a problem.

"It's just that my little Misha is locked up in our bedroom, and if you could take her for a short walk in the garden so she can tinkle . . ."

Misha was Alice's Yorkshire terrier, the tiniest mammal Wendy had ever seen, not counting mice, and Wendy adored him. "I'll be happy to walk him," she said, putting one final sprig of parsley on the cheese tray before nodding her approval. She could definitely use a breath of fresh air.

"When you get back, I'll introduce you to the guest of honor," Alice said. "He's probably not a good prospect for you—he and his wife are retiring in Tahiti or someplace—but he's got lots of friends."

Wendy wondered why she hadn't seen Captain Patterson yet. For a guest of honor, he sure was keeping a low profile.

"Hey, I thought you weren't coming," Joe said when he caught sight of Michael entering the drawing room at the mayor's mansion. "What changed your mind? Sharp tie."

Michael pulled at the tie in question. He'd bought a new shirt and tie that afternoon, though he wasn't sure why. Maybe he didn't want Wendy seeing him with all these hoity-toity people and noticing frayed cuffs.

"I'm here on business," he said. "James Batliner is on the guest list, and I'm going to collect some samples from him."

"Some sam—you mean hair, saliva, that kind of thing?" Joe's eyes widened. "You're in deep doo-doo if he catches you."

"He won't catch me. He's so gaga over his date that he won't notice if I stick him with a syringe and draw blood." He nodded toward James and his new conquest, an anorectic blonde with a flat chest and no color in her face. Under his breath, Michael muttered, "I can't believe he would prefer her over Wendy."

"Different strokes," Joe said. "I'll help you nail the guy. What do you want me to do?"

"See if you can spot a stray hair on his jacket," Michael said. "He's never met you, so he won't be suspicious if you tell him you're brushing lint off him. I'm going to nab his champagne glass—if he ever puts it down."

"Uh-oh, there he goes, toward the patio."

Michael started his way through the crowded room, enduring greetings and handshakes from several former coworkers he'd known when he'd worked patrol under Walt Patterson a zillion years before. He didn't want to appear anxious and alert his prey, yet he didn't want to lose sight of Batliner, either.

He'd just extricated himself from a particularly friendly female Internal Affairs detective when a vision across the room stopped him cold, then made him flush hot.

It was Wendy, holding a tiny dog and looking like some kind of sea nymph in a pale green dress that clung to her every lush curve. He fancied he could even make out the outline of her nipples through the clingy fabric. Then he realized he wasn't the only one watching her, and he experienced a flash of possessiveness that bordered on insanity. He'd never before wanted to throw a woman over his shoulder caveman fashion and haul her back to his lair, mark her with his brand.

He was about to tear himself away when she caught his gaze. They stared at each other for easily five seconds while time stood still and the room around him disappeared. Then she looked away, and the world righted itself again.

He had to talk to her, he decided. He had to confront her about her father and at least hear what she had to say about it.

One good thing: Wendy was about as safe as she could be. Who would bother her when she was surrounded by a hundred-plus cops?

The crowd shifted, and he lost sight of her. When it shifted again, it was clear she was gone from the room.

Michael made a mental note to look for her after he completed his mission. Then he planned to get out of this place and home to a cold beer and a basketball game on TV. A guy could take only so much small talk and teensy hors d'oeuvres.

James and his date had been heading toward the French doors and the patio when last Michael had seen them. He headed resolutely that way.

Outside, the air smelled like spring flowers mixed with chlorine from the lake-size swimming pool, but it was better than inside, where the overlay of aftershave and musky perfume was enough to turn his stomach. A country band was tuning up on the patio, and some of the younger guests were gathering there, anticipating some good two-stepping music.

Joe immediately approached him, his hand in the pocket of his trousers. "Hey. I've got a beauty of a two-inch blond hair from Batliner's collar. What should I do with it?"

"Good work. I've got plastic bags in my jacket."

"Hurry. I've got the darned hair clutched between my fingers, and I'm afraid I'll lose it."

"This way." They couldn't very well stand out in the open to bag evidence they were collecting illegally. The garden would provide them with some cover.

Behind a large arbor of wisteria, Michael transferred the single hair into a plastic bag, sealed it, and marked it with a permanent marker.

"You came prepared," Joe said. "Want me to try for the champagne glass? He's bound to put it down at some point, unless he's planning to pilfer it."

Michael couldn't help smiling as he pocketed the plastic bag. "Yeah, go for the glass. You're getting into this cloak-and-dagger stuff. Maybe you ought to apply for some undercover work."

"As long as I could get away with not wearing a tie." Joe strode off, intent on his mission. Michael took another breath, thinking maybe he'd stay out there, away from the insincere conversation and the slightly inebriated laughter. Most of the guys were there for the free food and booze. Captain Patterson was called Little Patton behind his back and hadn't endeared himself to many of his underlings.

Michael spotted a wisp of green cloth from the corner of his eye. He turned and saw Wendy walking the little dog on a leash. She had her back to him, tapping her foot while waiting for the dog to find a spot he liked. Michael took the opportunity to drink in the sight of her long neck, her bare, slender arms, and the way her dress cupped under her shapely bottom just slightly. Even the small slice of ankle showing at her hem was enticing.

She turned and caught him staring. He decided to brazen it out. "Wendy," he called, waving. "I'd like a word with you." This was as good a place as any to talk to her. At least they could speak without being overheard.

She nodded, then pointed toward a honeysuckle-encrusted gazebo. "I only have a minute." She scooped up the rodent-sized dog and led the way to the gazebo. He followed, his gaze riveted on her gently swaying hips and the way the shimmery dress draped around her legs.

They settled on separate benches in the gazebo.

The dog hopped off Wendy's lap and started to sniff all around, content for the moment to be ignored.

"The party is . . . great," Michael began, lamely, he thought. "You do good work."

"Thank you. I've met a couple of potential new clients. But I'm sure you don't want to talk about my work."

"No."

"Actually, I'm glad you're still speaking to me. I haven't been the most gracious . . . lover."

His heart beat faster at her use of that word, at the reminder of what they'd shared and what they should—must—put behind them.

"The truth is, I knew it was just a fling for you, so I—"

"How did you know that?" he broke in.

She shrugged, looking uncomfortable. "Seems to me you said as much. Anyway, you'll be going away soon. What else could it be but a fling?"

"Whether I'm going away or not is debatable at this point." He had considered withdrawing his application. Maybe he wasn't on the fast track in Dallas, but he enjoyed his work most of the time. He liked Joe, and he could work for worse men than Captain Rogers. Who knew what kind of people he'd have to put up with in Washington?

Then there was the snow and ice. He'd never shoveled a sidewalk in his life, and he wasn't keen on learning how.

But he couldn't tell Wendy he wasn't moving away after all, not until he was positive. He didn't want to give her the idea that *she* was the reason he wanted to stay.

"You'll do what you have to do, I'm sure," she said. But did he detect a note of hope in her voice? Did she really care whether he stayed or went? He'd been under the impression she didn't. "Have you got any new leads?" she asked.

He nodded. "I don't know whether it's good or bad for you, but I'm 99 percent sure James Batliner is involved."

Wendy closed her eyes, as if absorbing pain. "Do you think he went out with me just so he could hack into my computer?"

Michael shook his head. "I find that highly difficult to believe." In this low light he couldn't tell, but he thought she might be blushing. "The prosecutor will claim you two were in it together."

She sighed. "I can't seem to win. You finally corral another suspect and it only makes my situation worse."

"Your lawyer can put a favorable slant on things, I'm sure. He's good at that."

"Is that all you wanted? 'Cause I really need to get back—"

"No. I want to talk to you about your father."

She sighed again. "You found out about him."

"Your pal James spilled the beans," Michael said softly, suddenly feeling sorry for her. It must have been tough growing up with a father like that. Whatever her reasons for lying to him, he wanted to hear them. "It wasn't very gentlemanly of him. He was deliberately trying to cast guilt on you, which only made me suspect him more."

Wendy gnawed on her lower lip, which was what she did when she was nervous, he'd discovered. "I wanted to tell you," she said. "I didn't like lying. But it just looks so bad, me being the daughter of a habitual criminal. And I knew that once you found out, you'd be honor bound to reveal the truth. You would never lie for me."

"You're wrong. I would lie for you. Or, at least, I might not tell the whole truth."

She couldn't have looked more surprised if he'd announced he intended to strip naked and dance on the mayor's roof.

"I wouldn't lie about facts pertinent to the case, but in this instance, your family history has no bearing on the investigation. I see no reason to mention it in my report."

"Oh, Michael, thank you!" Before he knew what was happening, she'd launched herself at him, throwing her arms around his neck in a hug he was sure she meant to be wholly asexual. Unfortunately, his body didn't know the difference. He'd been wondering what it would feel like to press her curves, so blatantly displayed in that wisp of a dress, against him. Now he knew. And she couldn't help but notice what she did to him. Talk about blatant displays.

She pulled back a fraction to look into his eyes, and what he saw on her face was anything but asexual. "I'm sorry, Michael. I'm so sorry for leaving you when you were in the shower. I didn't do it to be mean. I was just scared and running from something that was about to overwhelm me," she said, the words rushing out in a jumble, "and I didn't know how I'd be able to handle it when you walked away, so I did it first."

He ran his hands up and down the whisper-soft fabric of her dress, then deliberately tangled his finger in her fiery hair. "You think too much."

That first touch of lips to lips was incredibly sweet, like a memory of some long-ago summer, eating homemade ice cream and watching fireworks on the Fourth of July, a good, good feeling of something so pleasurable, it almost hurts.

Then sweet gave way to a powerful, ripping hunger. Their breaths came fast as he plundered her mouth with his tongue and squeezed her bottom with both hands. Yes, he was remembering—the feel of her sweat-soaked limbs entwined with his in impossible configurations as they'd sought release in a half-dozen frantic positions.

"Oh, Michael." She said his name on a desperate groan. "I want you so bad even though I know it's wrong—"

He cut her off with a kiss. "It's not wrong. How could this be wrong? I want to be inside you."

"Here? What if someone sees us?"

"They won't," he said with more confidence than was warranted, because he was crazy with wanting her and he would do or say anything to have her. The Wendy Thayer Effect was now a proven fact. He'd never been so out of control in his life, and it scared the hell out of him. But it didn't scare him enough to make him stop. He pulled her dress up so he could feel the bare skin of her thighs and the silk of her panties. He groaned when he realized she wasn't wearing pantyhose. Just a scrap of silk separated him from the sweet recesses he so desired.

She laughed nervously, but the laughter turned into a moan as he slid his hand inside her panties to cup her bare bottom. He dipped his head under her chin to flick his tongue over the tops of her breasts. She rewarded him with a guttural sound that he wouldn't have believed could come from such a petite woman.

"All right," she said. "You win. But you're going to explain this—oh, yessss!—to the mayor if we get caught."

"Believe me, it's not going to last that long." He reached for his belt, unfastening it with one yank. Wendy took over from there, unfastening and unzipping his trousers. In moments she had freed him from the confines of his clothing. She grasped his arousal, and it was his turn to groan. He wanted to explode right then and there.

"It's now or never, sweets." He lifted her dress higher and bunched it around her waist, then slid her panties down to her knees.

"Can we do this standing up?" she asked, though she didn't resist at all when he bent his knees and brought her closer, preparing to enter paradise.

"I could do it on my head if that's what it took," he said, lifting her slightly, then impaling her.

Sweet heaven, he'd never felt anything like Wendy

all around him in their own garden of delights, the scent of honeysuckle heavy on the air, the buzz of insects serenading their dance of passion.

"Oh, Michael, I know this isn't the right time to tell you this, but I love you. I must. I would never act this crazy with someone I didn't love."

He stilled for just a moment and reveled in those words. He'd never imagined a woman's love could make him feel like such a . . . such a man.

"See, I knew I shouldn't have said anything."

"Shh," he said, moving inside her by pulling her against him with the most subtle of motions. He almost said it back. But he knew from experience that making a promise he couldn't keep was worse than keeping silent.

They spoke no more as their passions took complete control of them. Michael held back, prolonging their coupling longer than he'd predicted. But he'd be damned if he would take his pleasure before she'd enjoyed hers. And he knew from their night together that she would. He only hoped she could keep from screaming this time, or a hundred cops would come running to see who was being murdered.

When she reached her climax, he watched her face, enthralled at the rapture he saw there. Then she pressed her face into his shoulder and muffled her cries of ecstasy. His own peak of pleasure followed soon after. Only after he'd made one final thrust and released himself inside her did he realize they'd done it again. Like a couple of ignorant, horny teenagers, they'd forgotten to use any form of birth control.

He didn't care. He wanted her to bear his children, he thought with a rush of understanding. Why had he fought the feelings? So, he'd known her for less than a week. That was long enough. Screw the FBI. He'd stay in Dallas and make babies with Wendy.

He was about to tell her just that when he heard his name over the strains of country music coming from the patio, riding on the wind in a hoarse whisper. "Tagg? Hey, Tagg, where'd you go?"

If someone had been timing him and Wendy, they'd have won a world speed record in clothes-straightening. "That's my partner. Don't leave the party without me." He gave her one final kiss and left her in the gazebo to compose herself before facing the party guests.

ELEVEN

Wendy scurried upstairs and deposited Misha in the Munns' bedroom. He gave her a knowing look.

"Not a word to anyone, now," she admonished him before closing the door.

She was out of her mind to make love to Michael in the gazebo of the mayor's house. If they'd gotten caught, she would have lost every shred of credibility she'd possessed. But they hadn't gotten caught. Now she felt deliciously optimistic about her future. James, the creep, was involved in the crimes she'd been accused of. Once subjected to Michael's interrogation, James would sing like a canary on speed. Mr. Neff would be caught. And Michael had said his appointment to the FBI wasn't a sure thing.

Not that she would want him to be turned down, if that's the job he really wanted. But if his application was rejected, it wouldn't be all bad.

She took a quick tour around the downstairs. They

were getting low on plates, and guests were still arriving. She breezed into the kitchen, saw that the dishwasher was almost through its cycle, and nodded with satisfaction.

Alice came in right behind her. "Oh, Wendy, there you are. Misha must have taken you on some walk."

"Sniffed every blade of grass," Wendy said, hoping she wasn't blushing.

"Is everything going okay?"

"Fine." She and the head caterer both nodded.

"Have you checked the candles out front?"

Ah. She'd been caught neglecting her duties. "I'll go right now."

"Oh, it's okay. I want you to meet the guest of honor, Captain Walt Patterson." Alice took Wendy's arm and dragged her out of the kitchen. "Now, where did I see him? Oh, there, by the bar."

Wendy could see a small, wiry man standing at the bar, chatting up the bartender as he mixed a drink. Darn, she didn't have her business cards with her. Well, if he was at all interested, she could slip him one later.

"Captain Patterson?" Alice said. "I'd like you to meet the young lady responsible for planning and carrying out your party. Wendy Thayer."

The man turned. And Wendy found herself staring into the faded blue eyes of Barnie Neff. The gold tooth was gone, replaced by a good pair of dentures. The glasses were different, and he wore a toupee. But she wasn't in any doubt at all.

To his credit, he showed no surprise, no inappropriate reaction at all. Just a pleasant smile. "Well, it's nice to meet you, Miss Thayer." Wendy just stood there frozen as he shook her hand.

What should she do? My God, Mr. Neff was in the police department, a captain respected and revered by everyone! If she suddenly started shouting and pointing to him, accusing him of being a criminal, they would lock her away in an insane asylum.

She expected he knew this, as he didn't seem to be even slightly uncomfortable.

"Very nice party," Patterson said. Alice wandered away, secure that she'd done her duties as a hostess and that a friendly conversation was under way. "I'm sure Dallas's elite will miss you when you're gone."

She didn't miss the implied threat. Afraid she would make a scene, she simply turned on her heel and walked away, followed by Patterson's soft laughter.

So, he thought he held all the cards, did he? They would just have to see about that. She had to find Michael—now. He would know what to do.

Michael caught up with James again in the library, where he was sampling from the cheese tray while his date perused the titles of some old leather-bound volumes. The room wasn't crowded enough for Michael to lose himself, so he didn't go in. He sent Joe instead.

"Cheese," he said. "See if you can get a chunk of cheese after he's taken a bite."

"Whoa, this'll be fun," Joe said, slipping into the library.

Michael waited outside the door, pretending interest in some framed prints on the wall.

He sensed her before he saw her. Wendy. He was so in tune with her soul, he figured he could find her anywhere, like radar finding a lost plane.

"Wendy." His smile froze when he saw the stricken look on her face. "God, Wendy, what is it?"

"I saw Mr. Neff. He's here, at this party."

"Are you sure?"

She nodded emphatically. "I spoke to him. He knew I knew who he was, and he threatened me."

"Where is he?" Michael asked excitedly. "Point him out. I'll arrest him on the spot."

She didn't immediately follow him, so he stopped and turned back. "What?"

"He's a cop."

That gave him pause. The police chief was proud of the fact that his department hadn't exhibited even a whiff of scandal since he'd taken over. "Do you know his name?"

She nodded. "Captain Walt Patterson."

He froze, shocked to the core. "Are you sure?"

"I'm positive."

Michael didn't say anything for a moment, letting this sink in. A forty-year police veteran was a jewel thief and a housebreaker. That sounded crazy!

"Remember the name on the house and the utilities? Pat Walters? Walt Patterson? It fits, don't you see?

Michael was remembering something else. When he'd checked up on the owners of the brown Caprices, Walt Patterson's wife's name had come up. He and Joe had laughed about it. And the artist's composite. Joe had thought it looked like Patterson.

He should've seen the pattern. But who could possibly suspect Patterson and get away with it?

"Well?" Wendy asked, hands on her hips. "What are you waiting for?"

"I can't just waltz up to Captain Patterson and arrest him," he said, trying to be the voice of reason. "I have to go through channels. Arrests of this magnitude have to be taken one step at a time so later there's no way a defense attorney can get him off on a tech—"

"Michael, you can't wait. He knows I know. He could make his escape right now and be on a plane out of the country by midnight."

"Let me talk to my captain."

"I say you arrest now and talk later. Isn't that what you did with me? The man wants to kill me! You have to do something now!"

He recognized the note of hysteria in Wendy's voice, and he didn't blame her one bit. "You stay right with me and nothing will happen to you," he said reasonably. "I have to follow procedures."

Wendy was having none of his reason. "You're just afraid to take any risks because you don't want to jeopardize your freaking FBI job. Well, just forget it. I'll take care of this myself. I'm going straight to the mayor, and I'll bet *he* does something."

Michael debated about whether to let her go, finally deciding it couldn't hurt to come after Patterson from two fronts. Plus, he'd rather talk to his captain alone, without her panicked pleadings. Rogers was a logical man, and his first thought would be that Wendy, increasingly desperate over her impending conviction, was making a wild, groundless accusation. He would act against Patterson only after Michael laid out the evidence in an organized and compelling fashion.

With a determined gait, he headed toward the great hall where the main cluster of party guests lingered. He hoped Rogers would be there.

As soon as Taggert disappeared, Patterson stepped out from behind the potted palm where he'd been hiding himself. He'd heard the whole exchange. He wasn't too worried about Captain Rogers. Patterson had already told him that Taggert was lusting after their suspect and so couldn't be trusted. He was confident the good captain would never believe Taggert.

Wendy was the one who worried him. The mayor had a real soft spot for her, and though her accusation would seem outlandish, he wouldn't dismiss it out of hand without some type of investigation.

He couldn't allow Wendy to reach the mayor. Period.

Of all times for hizzonor to play coy! Wendy thought, annoyed. He'd been highly visible all night, gladhanding everyone in his path, paving the way for his next campaign. Now he seemed to have gone into hiding. Even Alice hadn't seen him.

"He was complaining of a headache earlier," Alice said. "Perhaps he went upstairs to find some aspirin. You can go up there to look for him if you want," she said amicably. "He won't mind. He's quite fond—"

She broke off as the country-and-western band on the patio started up with a raucous tune.

"Oh, my, they're loud," she said, raising her voice over the music and laughing.

"The younger folks will love it," Wendy assured her distractedly before breaking away. She wasted no time in heading for the stairs.

As she reached the second-floor landing, a strong arm reached out and grabbed her by the neck, yanking her around a corner so fast, her feet left the floor for an instant. She started to cry out in shock and fear, but a hand clamped over her mouth, making it impossible for her to breathe, let alone scream. Another hand twisted her arm behind her back, nearly dislocating her elbow.

Suddenly her fear was pushed aside by a pure, white-hot anger at the person who would do such violence to her—and she had no doubts as to his identity. Her body reacted instinctively. She twisted, she bit, she kicked backward. One of her spike heels came into contact with her attacker's shin, and she was rewarded with a grunt of pain. But he didn't loosen his hold on her one bit.

"Stop it!" Walt Patterson hissed in her ear. "Don't

make this any harder than it already is. I'm not going to hurt you. I just want to talk."

Wendy immediately recognized the lie. He would spend years in prison—maybe the rest of his life—if she lived to identify him; he knew that. He was going to finish the job he'd started two days before.

She fought him that much harder, but his hold on her was amazingly strong for a senior citizen's. She realized he was dragging her up another flight of stairs to the third floor, where their struggle wouldn't be heard by the party guests downstairs.

Even if she did manage to scream, she realized, no one would hear her over the blasted band.

Was this it, then? Was she about to die? Rather than panic her, the thought of her imminent demise filled her with a calm resoluteness. If ever there was a time she needed a clear head and all the ingenuity she could muster, this was it. As they reached the third-floor landing, she tried to think of ways she could convince Patterson *not* to kill her.

The most important of those reasons was that she would never get to see Michael again, never feel his arms around her or hear him tell her he loved her. But she didn't figure Patterson would give a rat's tail about that.

Tears sprang to her eyes, and she blinked them back.

Patterson never even broke stride as he dragged her down a long hallway. Wendy got the distinct impression he knew exactly where he was going, that he'd planned her murder in advance.

At the end of the hall was a set of French doors. Patterson had to remove his hand from across her mouth to turn the handle. That was the opportunity she'd been waiting for.

She didn't waste her time screaming. She started in with her logic. "You will *not* get away with this," she said. "I already told Michael Taggert that you're Barnie Neff. If you kill me—"

"But I'm not going to kill you," he argued reasonably. "After your lovers' quarrel with Sergeant Taggert—and given the hopelessness of your legal situation—you will throw yourself off the third-story balcony. Any accusations you made against me will be written off as completely insane, attributed to your increasing desperation to remain out of jail."

Damn. His arguments made way too much sense.

"You haven't killed anyone yet," she said. She was desperate, all right, though right now jail sounded infinitely preferable to Patterson's plans for her. "You could probably get a suspended sentence for the burglaries."

"You don't know much about criminal law, do you?"

"I won't tell anyone! I'll tell Michael I was mistaken about Neff's identity."

He didn't even honor that claim with a denial.

"Three stories isn't that far up," she tried again. "How do you know I'll die?"

"Because your neck will be broken before the fall. The medical examiner won't be able to tell when it happened."

His casual passing of her death sentence sent cold chills rippling up Wendy's back and into the roots of her hair.

"I'm sorry I can't, er, numb you ahead of time, to spare you the pain," he said. "But any drug I might use would be detected in your system, and that might lead to questions I don't want answered."

His show of compassion didn't fool her. The man was without a conscience. How had she ever thought this monster was a sweet old man? How could she have been fooled so thoroughly?

He had her on the balcony now. Far below were flagstones, hard as granite. She tried not to think about her bones shattering against the unyielding surface. Around the corner of the mansion, the hardiest of the party revelers danced to the country music. She could see a few of them as they drifted to the very edges of the patio, but none were looking her way.

She refocused her attention on Patterson. He was a coolheaded man of logic.

"Sergeant Taggert believed me when I told him you were Barnie Neff," she said, speaking quickly now, knowing she had only a few seconds in which to change her enemy's mind. "He'll know what really happened. He'll know I wasn't suicidal. You're only making your situation worse."

"It would take your Michael forever to convince anyone I'm guilty of jaywalking, much less murder. By the time he gets anyone to listen—and I don't think he will—I'll be in Tahiti."

"If they won't listen to him, why would they listen to me? You don't have to kill me!"

"Unfortunately, my dear, you have the mayor's ear. He'll believe you."

"No, he won't!" she shrieked as he pushed her up against the wall, preparing to do unspeakable violence to her.

"Oh, and Wendy," he said, his voice soft, almost seductive. "You don't look anything like my sister."

"Have you gone completely mad?" Captain Rogers asked Michael. "Walt Patterson, a jewel thief and housebreaker?"

They were on the patio, where even some distance from the band it was difficult to converse.

"I'm not saying he did it with his own two hands. But he's involved. He got Wendy involved, posing as this Mr. Neff character. Didn't you see how the composite drawing looked like him? The car that nearly ran Wendy over was registered to his wife."

"I thought you didn't get a complete license number on that car."

"I eliminated all but a handful of possibilities," Michael said, desperation creeping up on him. He'd known this story would go over like a lead balloon.

Rogers leaned closer and spoke loudly into Michael's ear to be heard over the band. "Look, Tagg, everybody knows you've got a thing for this girl. It happens. I'm not saying I don't frown upon it, but I didn't think you'd let it interfere with your judgment."

God, had he been that transparent, wearing his heart on his sleeve like a mooning teenager? He didn't bother denying he had a "thing," as the captain put it, for Wendy. "Look, Captain, I've gotten to know Wendy well enough in the past few days to know she's not making this up. Patterson is deep into this thing, and if we don't do something about it now, he'll be in Tahiti—or wherever he's *really* going—where we can't touch him."

"What are you proposing we do?" Rogers asked, arms folded. And mind closed, Michael imagined.

"Arrest him. Wendy's talking to the mayor even now. He'll believe her."

Rogers groaned. "That's just what I need. Okay, look. I wasn't going to tell you this until it was a sure thing, but the D.A. is going to drop the charges against Ms. Thayer. It looked like an open-and-shut case at first, but Nathaniel Mondell has introduced enough doubt, and with public opinion lined up squarely behind Ms. Thayer, the D.A.'s office just figured it wasn't worth it to prosecute. They'd like to pursue other suspects, like this James Batliner."

Michael shook his head. "That's great news. But that doesn't address the fact that Walt Patterson is trying to have Wendy killed because she's the only one who can identify him as Mr. Neff."

"Really, Tagg—"

The country band finished its number with an off-key guitar flourish, and blessed stillness took over. Other than a smattering of applause, it was relatively quiet again.

Michael lowered his voice, though his tone was even more insistent than before. "*Someone* is trying to kill her! Captain, if you've ever thought I had an ounce of common sense or reliable cop's instincts, think it now. We have to do something about Patterson, and we have to do it now—tonight—before—"

That's when he heard a scream in the distance, and it wasn't just a partyer with too much to drink. There was undeniable terror in that scream.

Judging from the expression on Rogers's face, he'd heard it too. "I'll go this way," he said, indicating the French doors. "You check outside."

Michael nodded his agreement and set out, scanning the grounds for some sign of movement.

It was impossible to say where the scream had come from. Michael made a three-sixty, trying to see everything at once. There! A flash of movement up on the third-floor balcony. He ducked behind an overgrown bush, then darted from bush to tree trunk to birdbath, hoping he wouldn't be seen.

When he got close enough to evaluate the situation, his heart jumped into his throat. Wendy, unmistakable in her body-hugging green dress, and a man struggled on the balcony.

Good God, Michael thought, he had to do something and fast. If she were to topple over that railing, she would die when she hit those solid flagstones. And that was only if her assailant didn't kill her first.

Michael saw no easy way up—no convenient trellises or trees with low branches. Only the exterior wall, made of rough-hewn Austin stone, offered any hope of access.

It would take him too long to go around. He leaped away from his cover and drew closer to the house. Three stories of sheer wall, straight up. But the cornices would work as footholds. And there was a puny ivy that might offer a handhold. He'd done some rock climbing once.

He kicked off his shoes and started the climb, working his way foot by foot, sometimes inch by inch, upward.

The band had started up again, but Michael could still hear Wendy screaming. Each shriek that tore from her throat made him die a thousand deaths. Could no one else hear her?

"You're tougher than you look," the assailant—definitely Captain Patterson—said. He was breathing hard. He wasn't a large man, and at sixty-five he'd probably lost some of the strength of his youth. Wendy apparently was holding her own against him.

Fight him off just a few seconds longer, Wendy, he silently begged. *I'm coming for you.*

Michael's head cleared the balcony floor, and he could see them now through the slats in the wooden railing. Patterson had hold of Wendy by the shoulders and was attempting to knock her against the stone wall. Michael realized the man's diabolical plan in an instant. He was going to beat her to death, then toss her over the railing, so it would look as if she'd jumped.

Michael grabbed onto the railing with one hand

just as his foothold gave way. He found himself dangling in thin air by one arm. That was when Wendy saw him.

Their eyes met for an instant. She let out an involuntary gasp, which was all it took to alert Patterson to Michael's presence.

Michael pulled himself even with the top of the railing and swung one leg up, trying to strengthen his precarious perch before Patterson could come after him. He had only a second or two. The old man, with the light of insanity burning in his eyes, turned away from Wendy and toward Michael.

Patterson stepped on Michael's hand where it extended through the railings.

"Damn it, Tagg, why couldn't you let it be? Now I'm going to have to kill you too."

Michael couldn't say anything through the haze of pain coming from his hand as Patterson casually crushed his fingers against the concrete balcony.

"Stop it!" Wendy grabbed Patterson's arm and tried to pull him off balance, but he shook her off. Wendy looked around frantically until her gaze fastened on a wire mesh hanging basket filled with petunias. In milliseconds it was in her hands. She bashed Patterson over the head with it.

The impact stunned him. He staggered, and Michael reclaimed his hand. Somehow, during those few seconds it took for Patterson to recover, Michael pulled himself fully to the top of the railing. Wendy grabbed onto his leg, then his arms and shoulders, and hauled him the rest of the way over.

"Michael, look out!"

Patterson was himself again. He immediately set upon Michael, grabbing him by the lapels of his jacket and pushing him backward against the railing. Michael hadn't had time to prepare for the attack. He couldn't find a handhold, could only flail at Patterson. He didn't dare kick and lose his tenuous grip on the balcony floor.

Wendy was on Patterson again, kicking with her spike heels and beating his head with her dainty fists. Her fighting style wouldn't win her many points, but she proved just enough of an annoyance that Patterson's concentration broke.

He pulled away from Michael to jab an elbow into Wendy's stomach, momentarily incapacitating her.

That break was all Michael needed. With a mighty push, he launched himself off the railing and toward Patterson, felling him with one body blow.

But Patterson wasn't about to give up. He tripped Michael with a scissors kick. Michael fell with an "Oof!" on top of the older man, and they rolled around on the concrete, neither really taking the advantage for long.

"Wendy, go get help," Michael ground out as Patterson got a hand around his throat.

She didn't budge, just stood there transfixed by the violent dance in front of her.

"Wendy!" He choked.

From the corner of his eye, he saw her go down.

"I'll see you in jail for the rest of your life for

assaulting a superior officer," Patterson said. "Don't think for a minute anyone will believe—"

The French doors burst open, and Captain Rogers leaped onto the balcony with two officers. "Freeze!"

Michael was more than happy to stop struggling. But Patterson, seeing no way out, gave one last mighty shove, pushing Michael through the flimsy railing and over the balcony.

During that split second when he teetered on the edge with nothing but empty space below him, Michael had a choice. He could either let go and fall to an uncertain fate, or take Patterson with him.

He chose to let go, but Patterson didn't. He clutched at Michael's jacket and allowed the momentum to pull him after Michael. Wendy's agonized "No!" followed them as they fell.

Wendy groggily opened her eyes. The first thing she noticed was a splitting pain in her head.

"There, she's coming to," a strange female voice said. A terrible smell invaded her nose. Her eyes flew open. She was lying on her back on the balcony, and a woman she'd never seen before bent over her with a vial of smelling salts.

"Michael?" she croaked. "Oh, God, he fell—" She tried to sit up, but the woman—a paramedic, Wendy realized—restrained her.

"Easy now. You're going to be fine."

But what about Michael? He'd fallen three stories. "Michael?" she said again, in a stronger voice. "Someone please tell me what happened."

"I'm right here." His voice was strong and sure. Relief flooded her, and she would have jumped for joy if she could have. Unfortunately, she was completely immobile, strapped onto a board of some kind. A big foam contraption around her head prevented her from even turning to look in his direction. But she felt it when he stroked her hand, distinctly recognized his touch from those of several strangers working on her.

"Sir, could you please move aside and sit down?" the paramedic said. "John, do something about this guy's arm."

His arm? What was wrong with his arm? "Michael, are you all right?"

He let go of her hand, but he remained near, talking to her. "I'm fine. You're going to be fine, too, you hear me?"

"Yes." She wanted to close her eyes and sleep, but she was afraid she would fall unconscious again. Her head felt like a walnut being cracked. "How did you . . ."

"I didn't fall all the way down. I caught myself on the second-floor balcony. Broke my arm, I think."

"You *think*?" someone said.

"And Patterson?" Wendy asked.

"He didn't die from the fall. They're working on him. But he confessed, Wendy. Before the ambulance got here, he told half a dozen witnesses that he and

James set you up and framed you. The charges against you will be dropped."

Damn, she thought. The man had had a shred of conscience after all. She tried to hate him, but all she could feel was pity, and sorrow for his wife. She couldn't even hate James, who'd played her for an incredible fool. She was too filled with relief that she and Michael had both survived.

After all she'd been through, the news that she'd been cleared seemed anticlimactic. She was almost disappointed. No more excuses to see Michael. Which was probably for the best, she thought glumly. He'd be going away soon.

"I'm sorry about your arm," she said. "That won't hurt your chances for the FBI, will it? I mean, they can wait a few weeks for you to start training, right?"

"It doesn't matter. I'm withdrawing my application first thing Monday morning."

Wendy didn't know what to say.

Michael stood up and leaned over her stretcher so she could see him, and she almost wished he hadn't. He looked as if he'd gone a few rounds with Mike Tyson. "Oh, Michael."

He ran one finger over her cheek in a caress as light as a butterfly's wings. "Wait till you see your own face, kiddo."

"Are you sure? About the FBI, I mean?"

"The Bureau's not important to me anymore. I'm happy with my job. I think I just needed a kick in the pants, a wake-up call to show me what's really important. And maybe someone to share the ups and downs with."

Tears sprang to her eyes. Was he saying what she thought he was?

"We're moving her now," the paramedic said.

"No, wait," Michael said urgently, "just one more second." He turned back to Wendy. "I love you, Wendy. No way could I go traipsing off to Quantico and leave you here."

She wished she could touch him, clasp his hand against her face or kiss his palm. She settled for words. "Oh, Michael, I love you too. When I saw you go over the edge of that—"

"Time's *up*," the now-annoyed paramedic said. Reluctantly Michael pulled his hand away. "Get well, Wendy. Soon as you're feeling up to it, I owe you a heckuva birthday celebration."

She didn't know how her heart could soar when her body hurt so badly, but she'd never been happier in her life.

"And then we're going to talk about getting you some self-defense training. You fight like a girlie-girl."

"I *am* a girlie-girl," she called as the stretcher was carried away. But his teasing didn't dampen her mood one bit. Michael Taggert loved her. That love surrounded her in a warm glow that mitigated her pains. She would recover in record time.

EPILOGUE

Wendy's thirty-first birthday was definitely better than her thirtieth. Michael, now her husband and a homicide lieutenant, took the day off and let her sleep late, then brought her breakfast in bed. He'd even included the traditional bud vase with a single rose and, of course, the paper.

"I stole the sports section," he said, "but I left all the shopping circulars intact. You can read them, but no coupon cutting. You promised to take the whole day off."

"I know." And she intended to keep that promise. Jillian had taken on more responsibility as Wendy's pregnancy neared term. Wendy could relax today, knowing everything at Born to Shop would run smoothly.

She sat up and propped some pillows behind her. But there was no way the breakfast tray would go over her lap. Her knees, maybe.

After a couple of attempts, Michael finally set the tray on the bedside table. "There."

She smiled at him. "This is wonderful, Michael. You still haven't told me what you want for your birthday dinner tonight." Her discovery that they shared the same birthday, that his thirty-fifth hadn't been any more fun than her thirtieth, had been a fun surprise.

He winked. "How about you, covered with whipped cream?"

"That's disgusting!" she objected, whacking him with the folded paper. A few months ago, maybe. But now that she was as big as a house—

She froze as a wave of pain rippled through her belly. "Oh, no," she murmured. "Not before I've had my breakfast in bed." She'd decided to go off the ridiculous diet her obstetrician had put her on, just for this one meal. She reached for a piece of bacon and smiled up at Michael as she crunched it. "Mmm, delicious."

"What's wrong?"

"Nothing."

"You look funny."

Bill and Ted jumped on the bed together and started rubbing at Wendy's arm. She scratched them both behind the ears. "Nothing's wrong." She took another bite of bacon and promptly doubled over.

"Wendy!"

"Looks like we're going to have a third Taggert birthday to celebrate today," she said as calmly as she dared.

———❖————————❖———

Seven hours later, after a lot of cursing and panting and ice chips, Wendy gave one final push, and their baby came into the world. Michael watched the miracle happening, and he thought it was even better than when Maggie Courtland's baby had been born.

"It's a girl!" the doctor crowed, though Wendy and Michael had known the baby's sex for months. Still, the reality was so much better than the anticipation. The baby squalled its first, Wendy laughed and cried, and Michael hugged her gently. She'd been a trouper through the agonizing labor, and he'd been thanking every deity he could think of that he'd been born male.

Now the struggle was over, though. The doctor laid the incredibly tiny baby girl on Wendy's stomach. She touched it cautiously, her eyes full of wonder.

One of the delivery nurses looked on, grinning. "She's beautiful. What are you going to name her?"

Wendy and Michael looked at each other. "Consequences," they said together, then laughed giddily. Truthfully, they hadn't been able to decide on a name yet.

"Connie for short?" the nurse asked, playing along.

Connie. Yeah, that wasn't bad, Michael mused. From Wendy's thoughtful expression, he imagined she was thinking the same thing.

"Constance?" Wendy said, and Michael nodded. Constance was perfect. Their daughter's name would stand for the constancy of the love that had brought her into the world, the love that had sustained her parents through months of the painful aftermath following Patterson's death—he'd survived only a few hours—and James Batliner's prosecution.

Michael knew that love would sustain them through the rest of their lives. He brushed Wendy's hair from her face, then kissed her softly. "Constance," he murmured, and the baby squalled her approval.

THE EDITORS' CORNER

With Halloween almost over, Thanksgiving and Christmas are not far behind, and we hope the following four books will be at the top of your shopping list. It's not often that you can find everything you need in one store! All these sexy heroes have a special talent, whether it's rubbing the tension from a woman's shoulders or playing the bagpipes. You may just want to keep these guys around the house!

Cheryln Biggs presents **THIEF OF MIDNIGHT**, LOVESWEPT #910. When Clanci James stepped into the smoky bar, she'd already resigned herself to what she was about to do—find sexy Jake Walker, seduce him, drug him, and kidnap him. The creep was the one sabotaging her ranch, her grandfather was sure of it. So, while he looked for clues to incriminate Jake, Clanci had to keep him out of the way. When Jake comes to, he's alone, got a heck of a hangover, and he's tied to Clanci's bed. Insisting he's not the one who's kidnapped her horse, he promises to help a suspicious Clanci. As the search for the missing horse continues, Clanci and Jake are confined to close quarters, a situation that quickly reveals their real feelings. Clanci's been through love turned bad . . . will she throw caution out the window to chance love again? Cheryln Biggs throws a feisty cowgirl together with the rugged rancher next door.

A **FIRST-CLASS MALE** is hard to find, but in LOVESWEPT #911 Donna Valentino introduces Connor Hughes to one Shelby Ferguson, a woman in need of a good man. Connor is faced with two hundred hungry people and a miserable tuna casserole big enough to feed maybe fifty, at one noodle apiece. Apparently it *is* his problem when people show up to a potluck dinner without the potluck. So, when Shelby arrives with the catering vans, Connor knows his guardian angel is working overtime. Shelby's sister just got dumped at the altar, and there's enough food to feed, well, a hungry potluck crowd. Scared of the Ferguson curse that's haunted her all her life, Shelby won't risk her heart for anything but a sure thing. And if that means a staid but secure man, then so be it. But nowhere does it say she *has* to help out this seemingly unreliable guy. Never one to desert a person in need, Shelby offers to help Connor out in restoring Miss Stonesipher's house. Donna Valentino charts a splendidly chaotic course that will lead to a terrifically happy ending.

Jill Shalvis gives us the poignant **LEAN ON ME**, LOVESWEPT #912. Desperate to escape her old life, Clarissa Woods walked into The Right Place knowing that the clinic would be her salvation. Little did she know that its owner, Bo Tyler, would be as well. Bo has his own battles to fight, and fight he does, every day of his life. But his hope is renewed when he sets eyes on Clarissa. No one had ever treated Clarissa with kindness and compassion, but when she returns it, he still has his doubts. Together they work toward making his clinic a success, but will they take time to explore their special kinship? Jill Shalvis celebrates the heart's astonishing capacity for healing when she places one life in the hands—and heart—of its soul mate.

Kathy Lynn Emerson wows us once again in **THAT SPECIAL SMILE**, LOVESWEPT #913. Russ didn't know when his daughter had chosen to grow up, but he was definitely going to kill the woman who'd convinced her to enter the Special Smile contest. When he realizes that Tory Grenville is none other than Vicki MacDougall from high school, he coerces her to chaperon Amanda in the pageant. Tory doesn't really know anything about being in beauty pageants. At Amanda's age, she hadn't yet grown into her body, or gained the confidence only adulthood can give. But Russ is determined, and a guilty Tory can't very well say no. She teams up with Russ to get Amanda through the pageant, but when he starts to take an interest in her as a woman, Tory knows she's in trouble. Russ the school jock was one thing, but Russ the handsome heartthrob is another. Kathy Lynn Emerson offers the irresistible promise that maybe a few high school dreams can come true.

Happy reading!

With warmest wishes,

Susann Brailey   Joy Abella

Susann Brailey
Senior Editor

Joy Abella
Administrative Editor

P.S. Look for these women's fiction titles coming in November! *New York Times* bestselling author Sandra Brown brings us the timeless Christmas story **TIDINGS OF GREAT JOY.** Ria Lavender couldn't deny she wanted Taylor MacKenzie, the ladykiller with the devil's grin, but there's danger in falling for a man she can't keep. The enchantment begun in THE CHALICE AND THE BLADE continues in **DREAM STONE** as Glenna McReynolds weaves another strand in her incredible tale of romance, adventure, and magic. National bestseller Patricia Potter brings us **STARFINDER,** the enthralling, heartfelt love story of a Scotsman and a widow caught in a web of passion and danger in colonial America. In **THE PROMISE OF RAIN,** Shana Abé delivers a tale of a woman running from a murder at King Henry's court, the handsome, relentless man sent to bring her back, and the island where their secrets are revealed—an island that just might be as enchanted as their love. Finally, Juliana Garnett presents **THE SCOTSMAN.** A fiery Scottish rebel kidnaps the daughter of the English earl who holds his brother. But he soon discovers that the woman he has stolen from her family has stolen his heart. And immediately following this page, preview the Bantam women's fiction titles on sale in October.

For current information on Bantam's women's fiction, visit our website at the following address: **http://www.bdd.com/romance**

AN UNIDENTIFIED SKULL . . .
A TRAIL OF TERRIFYING SECRETS . . .
AND A WOMAN WHOSE
TALENTED HANDS
HOLD THE TRUTH BEHIND THE MOST
SHOCKING DECEPTION OF OUR TIME . . .

From Iris Johansen, the nationally acclaimed *New York Times* bestselling author of *And Then You Die* and *The Ugly Duckling*, comes her most electrifying novel yet, a relentless buildup of suspense from the first page to the riveting conclusion.

THE FACE OF DECEPTION

by Iris Johansen

Forensic sculptor Eve Duncan has a rare—and bittersweet—gift. Her unique ability to reconstruct the identity of the long dead from their skulls has helped bring closure to parents of missing children. For Eve, whose own daughter was murdered and her body never found, the job is a way of coming to terms with her personal nightmare.

When she is approached by John Logan to reconstruct the face of an adult murder victim, only his promise of a sizable charitable contribution persuades her to accept. It's a simple bargain, yet it's the most dangerous one she'll ever make.

The warning signs are clear. There is the specially equipped lab Eve is taken to, in a country inn turned high-tech security fortress in rural Virginia. Surveillance cameras monitor her every move. The telephones are tapped. And then there is Logan himself—by turns ruthless, charming, and desperate.

But it's too late for Eve to walk out. The skull has begun to reveal its shocking identity, trapping her in a frightening web of murder and deceit. To free herself, she has no choice but to expose that identity and to trust Logan, the man who put her life in danger, a man who may see her as an expendable pawn.

Already she has made very powerful enemies. Their only agenda is covering up the truth, and their method of choice is cold-blooded killing. To them, Eve needs to be silenced forever. Because the secret of the skull must remain in the grave—no matter who gets buried with it.

They were the perfect husband and wife—
until they fell in love

MERELY MARRIED

by Patricia Coughlin

Life for Adrian Devereau, the sixth duke of Raven, was flawless, but for one nagging detail. Try as he did to live down to his reputation as the Wicked Lord Raven, the ladies persisted in viewing him as desirable husband material. So he conceived a bold solution to foil them once and for all—he would marry a woman on her deathbed and adopt the role of grieving widower. He even found a most suitable wife: Leah Stretton, overtaken by a sudden illness while journeying to London. But with Leah's "miraculous" recovery, Adrian found himself properly wedded to a beauty as headstrong as she was healthy. Now his only chance at freedom was playing her game. More adept at writing about romance and adventure than living it, Leah could not permit a new family scandal to ruin her sister's launch into society. If Adrian played her devoted husband, she would grant him an annulment later. There was only one rule: neither of them could fall in love. Of course, rules were made to be broken.

Adrian was still savoring the praise being heaped on him by his guests when the crusty manservant who managed his household appeared by his side.

"What is it, Thorne?" he asked.

Thorne bent to whisper close to his ear. "A problem, sir. You ought—"

"You handle it," ordered Adrian, reluctant to have his amusement interrupted.

"Yes, sir. But you really ought to—"

"Not now, Thorne."

The servant set his jaw and glared at Adrian.

Adrian glared back. He understood that formal entertaining was a rarity in Raven House and a bloody strain on everyone, but Snake, the former infantryman who passed for a cook, had turned out an edible meal and a pair of feckless footmen had managed to relay it to the table with a minimum of mishaps. The least the old crank could do was *pretend* to be proper and heedful.

Instead he continued to glare. "What I am trying to say to you, Y'Grace, is—"

"Raven? Darling?" a woman's voice called from somewhere outside the dining room.

Darling?

Adrian registered the gleam of smug satisfaction in Thorne's squinty eyes just before the same intriguing female voice spoke again, this time from just inside the dining room.

"There you are." The woman threw open her arms and smiled at him as if they were alone. "Surprise, darling, I'm home."

Adrian gaped at her, frozen in his seat even as the other gentlemen at the table leapt to their feet. It was she. Leah. *His wife*.

Oh sweet Lord.

What was she doing standing in his dining room?

Hell, what was she doing *standing* anywhere?

She was supposed to be . . . well, dead.

He placed his palms flat on the table and pushed himself upright on leaden legs, only distantly aware of the expectant hush all around him.

This woman was most definitely not dead.

She was breathtakingly alive. With hair the color of blazing chestnuts and eyes like fields of clover. My God, his wife was a beauty.

His wife.

Oh sweet Lord, what the bloody hell was he going to do now?

He squared his shoulders, his usually quick wits slowed by shock. Instinct made him certain of only two things. First, if Leah Stretton was standing there calling him "darling" and apparently presenting herself as his wife, he'd damn well better start acting like a husband in a hurry. And second, when he got his hands on Will Grantley, England was going to be minus one inept, disloyal botchbag of a rector.

"Leah. My sweet," he said, forcing his facial muscles to form a smile. "You have taken me totally by surprise."

"Good." She captured his gaze and held it. "That was my intent."

The look she gave him left no doubt that she had meant to ambush him with her sudden appearance and was enjoying his discomfiture to the hilt.

But why?

Why indeed, he thought, recovering his senses. He should probably count himself lucky she'd come alone—and unarmed. Belatedly it occurred to him to wonder if the woman had brothers. Large brothers. Belatedly it occurred to him to wonder any number of things he should have considered a fortnight ago.

At the moment, however, his first order of business was to wipe the increasingly speculative looks from the faces of their audience.

Striding across the room, he grasped Leah by her shoulders. "God, how I've missed you. When you first walked in I thought I must be seeing things . . . that loneliness had driven me mad and you were but an apparition. But now . . ." He ran his hands down her arms, then up, finally sliding them around to her back to draw her closer and press her stiff body tightly to his. She blinked rapidly, signaling a crack in her composure.

Good, thought Adrian. Spring herself on him, would she?

"Now that I am convinced you are real, my own flesh-and-blood Leah," he went on, "I must do what I have been dreaming of doing since I left you in Devon what seems like years ago."

Their gazes remained locked as he lowered his head. He saw resistance flash in her eyes and felt it in her tensed muscles, but she didn't flinch or try to pull away. Had she, his urge to conquer might have been satisfied and he might have gone easy on her. As it was, he tightened his grip and opened his mouth, using his tongue to claim her the way any randy bridegroom would want to, but would doubtless restrain himself from doing before onlookers.

Adrian seldom restrained himself, and he certainly wasn't about to start now and give this presumptuous chit the notion that she had the upper hand. He kissed her hard and long, nearly forgetting that they were not alone and that it was merely a performance. His blood heated rapidly and one of his hands moved to rest on the pleasing curve of her hip, as naturally as if he had every right in the world to put it there.

When he finally remembered himself, he lifted his head slowly, watching her long, dark lashes flutter and open.

"Westerham," she said, her tone steady and audible enough for everyone in the room to hear.

Adrian frowned. "What did you say?"

"I said you left me in Westerham, not Devon. Have you forgotten already?"

Westerham. Saint Anne's. The rectory. Of course. Devon was where her *fictional* sister lived. But she had no way of knowing that, or the countless other details about her life that he had fabricated that evening. That could be a problem.

Could be a problem? He nearly laughed out loud at his own absurdity. This entire affair was turning into a debacle right before his eyes.

"No, no, of course I haven't forgotten," he assured her gently. "Though when you are close to me, it is a wonder I can even remember to breathe."

"Don't worry, darling, if you forget I'll prompt you. I happen to be a most accomplished breather."

"Yes, I can see that," he murmured, aware of the impudent glint in her eyes as she gazed up at him with seeming adoration. He released her and turned to his guests. "Please forgive my lapse in manners. I totally forgot myself for a moment."

Sir Arthur raised his hand. "Perfectly understandable under the circumstances, Raven. Think nothing of it."

"Yes, allowances must be made for newlyweds," his wife chimed in, her eyes as bright as those of a hound circling a meaty bone. "Especially when they have been separated for so long. But now, Raven, I insist you make us acquainted with this surprise addition to our party."

"Of course." He handled the introductions as succinctly as possible. Try as his overtaxed brain did, it could not come up with any way to avoid using the words *my wife* in presenting her. Though the phrases *long-lost sister* and *recently acquired ward* did flit through his mind.

The damage was done now. The best he could hope for was to limit the repercussions as much as possible. To that end he proceeded to push the chairs nearest him back to the table before any of his guests could resettle themselves.

"I know you'll understand if I beg to end the evening prematurely," he said when they persisted in lingering, inquiring about Leah's health and her journey to town, precisely the things he intended to inquire about the instant he had her alone. "I fear if sh . . . Le . . . *my wife* overtaxes herself she will suffer a relapse."

His wife slipped her arm through his. "Your concern is touching, darling, but altogether unnecessary. The doctor assures me that kidney stones rarely afflict women my age and a recurrence is unlikely."

Stones? thought Adrian.

"Stones?" exclaimed Lady Hockliffe. "Is that what ailed you? Why, you poor dear, that is a horror." She swiped at Raven with her closed fan. "You beastly man. If I were your bride I should never forgive you for abandoning me in my hour of need."

"I shall spend the rest of my life making amends," vowed Adrian, kissing the back of Leah's hand before tucking it inside his arm once more. Gently. There would be time later to squeeze the truth out of her.

THE LIGHT IN THE DARKNESS

by brilliant newcomer

Ellen Fisher

It was a complete joke to Grey that he was considered such a catch. Embittered by the death of his wife, scornful of female wiles, and completely contemptuous of any attempt to bring happiness into his life, Grey hardly considered himself good husband material. And yet, if only for the shock value of it—and to put an end to all the nagging—Grey showed up one day with a bride on his arm: an ignorant, ill-kempt, timid young tavern wench. . . .

Jennifer knew she was no one's idea of a suitable bride for the rich, elegant Grey—least of all, his. But though she couldn't begin to understand the reasons behind his caustic, tormented personality, she did know one thing. He had saved her from a life of drudgery and cruelty, and she would repay him by turning herself into a ravishing, accomplished beauty who would do him credit in society's eyes. And maybe, just maybe, in the process, he might fall in love with her just a little. . . .

Jennifer found herself lying awake in the darkness that night, completely unable to sleep. Her husband had finally noticed her, had even looked at her with something resembling new-found respect and admiration.

And now that he had noticed her, now that she had earned his attention, possibly, just possibly, he might begin to feel some sort of affection for her. Perhaps the time for Grey to mourn was finally over. Perhaps, at long last, it was once again time for him to love.

With these hopeful thoughts racing in her mind, she could not sleep. The music of the stars was calling to her. Slipping from her bed and pulling on a loose linsey-woolsey gown which did not require stays, she glided silently downstairs, only to pause at the sight of flickering candlelight in Grey's study.

"Grey?"

She moved closer to the door, seeing that his head was buried in his hands, his shoulders shaking. The words he had written to his deceased wife, Diana, darted through her mind, and she felt a slash of pity for her husband, so lost by himself but so completely unable to ask others for guidance.

Last time she had discovered Grey thus, she had only dared to peer around the edge of the door. This time, moved by an impulse she could not explain, she crossed the chamber swiftly and placed a hand on his shoulder. "Grey!" she whispered urgently. "It's all right. I'm here now."

Slowly he lifted his head, raking her face with his gaze. What she saw in his stormy gray eyes caught at her heart. Defeated, haunted, they were the eyes of a dying man.

"Don't cry," she murmured, brushing the tears from his haggard face as though he were a child. Strange, she thought, how he could be so arrogant and remote by day, yet so terribly vulnerable by night. "Don't."

"I can't help it," Grey muttered in a voice clogged to hoarseness by tears. As if embarrassed by her clear, level gaze, he lowered his face into his hands once more.

She stroked the thick black hair as he bowed his head in abject misery, wishing she could do more to ease his pain. "You mustn't feel this way," she said softly, aware that her words were woefully inadequate in the face of his agony. "Please . . ."

Grey looked up at her through red-rimmed eyes. "Ah, God," he said tiredly. "You're right. I should feel nothing, but I'm too full of emotion. All I can feel is love and sorrow and grief, churned together and swirling inside of me until I choke on it." He clutched her hand to his cheek in a gesture so childlike that a lump came to her throat.

In a moment some of his pain seemed to fade. He looked up in a way that was almost shy and studied her features in the candlelight. She thought there was something strange about the way he looked at her; his expression was intent but oddly blank, as though he were looking through her somehow. "You're very beautiful," he said at last. "Did you know that?"

Startled and shocked by his sudden mercurial change of emotions, Jennifer flushed a brilliant red and started to back away, but he caught her arms in a surprisingly strong grip. "Don't go," he pleaded in a desperate, low voice. The agony had faded from his features, replaced by something even more elemental. "I need you. You are so beautiful . . ."

She sensed that he was dreadfully drunk, but she could not pull away. His long fingers held her arms so tightly and his hopeful silver eyes held her pinned. "Grey," she said in what she hoped was a reproving tone. "Let go of me."

"I can't," Grey whispered. One of his hands released her arm and reached up to stroke the smooth curve of her jaw. Jennifer froze at the peculiar sensation of his strong, callused fingers caressing her soft skin. "I've tried, but I can't. I can never let go of you. Oh, God, I want you. And you want me too. Please tell me so."

She could not look into those brilliant silver eyes and lie. "I do," she admitted faintly. Heaven help her, it was true. There was something so blatantly masculine about him, clad as he was in a ruffled linen shirt that was open at the neck, exposing part of the solidly muscled expanse of his chest. There was something terribly compelling about his sharply chiselled features, thrown into sharper relief than ever by the faint light of the candle. Grey was more than attractive, more than handsome. He was irresistible.

"Say it," he commanded softly, eyes gleaming with something more than hope. Jennifer saw the powerful emotion in his eyes, recognized it for what it was with feminine instinct, and helplessly responded to it.

"I want you," she whispered, less shyly now.

The expression of raw, elemental passion on his face left little doubt that he returned the sentiment in full. How he could want her so powerfully, so desperately, when he had rarely even acknowledged her presence in the past she could not fathom, but it was evident that he did. She was unable to bring herself to question fate. Slightly dazed at the direction events were taking, she repeated, "I want you."

The crystalline truth of those words shocked her. She had thought herself attracted to his younger self, a man with Grey's arrogance and charm, but with Edward's passion. Somehow that man was before her now. He came slowly to his feet, staring down at her with all the passion that was his nature etched clearly on his handsome face.

And Jennifer felt the first passion of her life welling up in response. She did not struggle when his lips touched hers. The thought of struggle never occurred to her. Instead she responded eagerly, joyfully, wrapping her arms ardently around his broad shoulders, revelling in the strangely delightful sensations his caressing hands and lips aroused. Even when his lips opened and his tongue delicately stroked hers, she did not recoil in shock, only pressed herself closer to him. The taste of apple brandy on his lips was so intoxicating, his arms around her so warm and solid, that she wondered dizzily if she were dreaming. It had to be a dream. Reality had never been this wonderful.

On sale in November:

TIDINGS OF GREAT JOY
by *Sandra Brown*

DREAM STONE
by *Glenna McReynolds*

STARFINDER
by *Patricia Potter*

HEAR NO EVIL
by *Bethany Campbell*

THE PROMISE OF RAIN
by *Shana Abé*

THE SCOTSMAN
by *Juliana Garnett*

Bestselling Historical Women's Fiction

⚬AMANDA QUICK⚬

____28354-5 SEDUCTION ...$6.50/$8.99 Canada

____28932-2 SCANDAL ....$6.50/$8.99

____28594-7 SURRENDER ....$6.50/$8.99

____29325-7 RENDEZVOUS ......$6.50/$8.99

____29315-X RECKLESS ....$6.50/$8.99

____29316-8 RAVISHED ....$6.50/$8.99

____29317-6 DANGEROUS ....$6.50/$8.99

____56506-0 DECEPTION ....$6.50/$8.99

____56153-7 DESIRE ....$6.50/$8.99

____56940-6 MISTRESS ....$6.50/$8.99

____57159-1 MYSTIQUE ....$6.50/$8.99

____57190-7 MISCHIEF ....$6.50/$8.99

____57407-8 AFFAIR ....$6.99/$8.99

⚬IRIS JOHANSEN⚬

____29871-2 LAST BRIDGE HOME ...$5.50/$7.50

____29604-3 THE GOLDEN

           BARBARIAN ....$6.99/$8.99

____29244-7 REAP THE WIND ......$5.99/$7.50

____29032-0 STORM WINDS ....$6.99/$8.99

Bestselling Historical Women's Fiction

⚸ IRIS JOHANSEN ⚸

____28855-5 THE WIND DANCER . . .$5.99/$6.99

____29968-9 THE TIGER PRINCE . . .$6.99/$8.99

____29944-1 THE MAGNIFICENT

              ROGUE . . . .$6.99/$8.99

____29945-X BELOVED SCOUNDREL .$6.99/$8.99

____29946-8 MIDNIGHT WARRIOR . .$6.99/$8.99

____29947-6 DARK RIDER . . . .$6.99/$8.99

____56990-2 LION'S BRIDE . . . .$6.99/$8.99

____56991-0 THE UGLY DUCKLING. . .$6.99/$8.99

____57181-8 LONG AFTER MIDNIGHT.$6.99/$8.99

____57998-3 AND THEN YOU DIE.... $6.99/$8.99

⚸ TERESA MEDEIROS ⚸

____29407-5 HEATHER AND VELVET .$5.99/$7.50

____29409-1 ONCE AN ANGEL . . . . . .$5.99/$7.99

____29408-3 A WHISPER OF ROSES .$5.99/$7.99

____56332-7 THIEF OF HEARTS . . . . .$5.50/$6.99

____56333-5 FAIREST OF THEM ALL .$5.99/$7.50

____56334-3 BREATH OF MAGIC . . . .$5.99/$7.99

____57623-2 SHADOWS AND LACE . . .$5.99/$7.99

____57500-7 TOUCH OF ENCHANTMENT.$5.99/$7.99

____57501-5 NOBODY'S DARLING . . .$5.99/$7.99

- -

Ask for these books at your local bookstore or use this page to order.

Please send me the books I have checked above. I am enclosing $____ (add $2.50 to cover postage and handling). Send check or money order, no cash or C.O.D.'s, please.

Name _____

Address _____

City/State/Zip _____

Send order to: Bantam Books, Dept. FN 16, 2451 S. Wolf Rd., Des Plaines, IL 60018
Allow four to six weeks for delivery.
Prices and availability subject to change without notice.　　　　　FN 16 9/98